FORT BLOOD

FORT BLOOD

PONY SOLDIERS

CHET CUNNINGHAM

Thorndike Press • Chivers Press
Waterville, Maine USA   Bath, England

This Large Print edition is published by Thorndike Press, USA and by Chivers Press, England.

Published in 2002 in the U.S. by arrangement with Chet Cunningham.

Published in 2002 in the U.K. by arrangement with the author.

U.S. Hardcover 0-7862-3810-0   (Western Series Edition)
U.K. Hardcover 0-7540-4788-1   (Chivers Large Print)

The text of this Large Print edition is unabridged.
Other aspects of the book may vary from the original edition.

Set in 16 pt. Plantin by Rick Gundberg.

Printed in the United States on permanent paper.

British Library Cataloguing in Publication Data available

ISBN: 0-7862-3810-0

FORT BLOOD

CHAPTER ONE

Lieutenant Colonel Colt Harding could smell the Cheyenne from where he sat on his horse leading C Troop up the gentle valley in southern Wyoming.

His nose wrinkled as he looked around, every nerve in his body alert to the slightest noise or movement that would signal the hostiles starting a charge. They were out there somewhere in this small valley that led up to the ridge line of the foothills of the Larson mountains north and east of Larson City.

Colt Harding stood just a little over six feet tall and weighed 185 pounds. He was lean and fit, almost wiry, with short cropped brown hair, brown eyes under heavy brows. He wore a thick, full moustache trimmed on the sides, which helped him to look a little older than his 32 years.

He had been in the army all his adult life and now knew that something was wrong. He had smelled enough, fought with enough, and shot enough Indians in the past three years to last a lifetime, but he knew there would be lots more coming. Colonel Harding glanced over at the First Lieutenant who rode beside him. He seemed to be staring straight ahead.

Lieutenant Strachey was 24 years old, polished, a better educated man than most army officers, and had impressed Colt his first few days at this new post in Fort Larson. Strachey was about five-nine, slightly overweight, with a reddish face that did not tan well. His blue eyes could be cold. A shock of nearly blonde hair crowned his head.

Colt had arrived here two weeks ago as Commanding Officer, had his permanent rank raised to light colonel, and had been able to bring his family along. Fort Larson was right on the railroad, had a telegraph and all the comforts of home.

As Colt watched Lieutenant Strachey, he became more and more nervous. For a second Colt almost took command of the troop. It was time to stop and send out a scout or reconnoiter, to find out for sure what was going on out there, and far past time to watch for a trap.

First Lieutenant Rodney Strachey seemed mesmerized by the scenery. It was as if he wasn't paying any attention to the situation. Colt held himself in check. There was still time. He didn't like the way the sides of the small valley were covered with fir and spruce, making ideal cover. Those woods could be hiding 200 Cheyenne warriors, painted and ready for battle.

First Sergeant Theodore Troob rode on the other side of Troop C's Commanding Officer. He looked up at Strachey now, his forehead creased, his eyes squinting through his own frown. Colt saw the sergeant look over the terrain again and at the heavily forested slopes now starting to edge behind them on both sides. He cleared his throat and looked at the Lieutenant.

"Lieutenant, sir. This situation doesn't look good." He waved at the cover on both sides. "Could be a couple hundred Cheyenne on each side waiting for us in there. We could be riding right into a trap they laid for us."

First Lieutenant Strachey jolted as if coming awake. He looked first at his company's top sergeant, then at the sides and the trail that led forward up the slight grade. He held up his hand and the troop stopped. The men trailed along four abreast behind him for a total of 45 troopers.

Strachey stared at the forested sides of the valley, then at his men. He looked at his sergeant with a puzzled expression that was just short of a hysterical laugh.

"Sergeant, do you think. . . ." Strachey

stopped. "I mean, there could be some. . . ." Again he halted, the sentence unfinished. His head began to turn toward Colt, but stopped. "Well, Sergeant Troob, let's pull in the outriders and reconsider this."

Sergeant Troob gave a hand signal on one side, then on the other, and two outriders within 30 yards of the forested sides of the hills turned and galloped back to the troop.

Sergeant Troob was a compact man standing little over five feet six, with raven black hair, dark piercing eyes, a full beard and moustache which he kept trimmed at no more than a half inch. He was meticulous about his uniform and equipment, a strict disciplinarian, and went about his army duties as if they were the most important work in the world. Colt had liked the man at once. Colt had not figured out his age. Somewhere between 30 and 35, Colt guessed.

"Now then, let's see about this," Lieutenant Strachey said, looking ahead, then at both sides. When he turned to Colt there was the puzzled expression again, his eyes laughing already, his face starting to shatter into a giggle.

"Sir, I'd suggest we pull back before we reconnoiter. We don't want to get surrounded in there," Sergeant Troob said quietly.

"Uh! Oh, yes, Troob, good idea, let's do a

reverse march and get the hell some distance. . . ."

Just then a rifle barked from the trees 300 yards to their left and a cavalry mount shrilled in pain behind them. On that signal 50 Cheyenne warriors kneed their mounts out of the woods on the left and rode hard, straight for Troop C.

Sergeant Troob looked at his Commanding Officer, then without hesitation he bellowed: "Line of skirmishers to the left, MOVE!"

The four-deep horsemen smartly turned into a single line facing the oncoming hostiles and lifted rifles out of boots or retaining rings. The Cheyenne were still 250 yards away. Half the troopers had Spencer repeating carbines, the rest Sharps .50-70 carbines converted from percussion.

Colt looked at Lieutenant Strachey. He stared straight ahead, not even looking at the enemy on his left. His hands held his reins. He hadn't moved into the troop front as Sergeant Troob had. Colt shook his head and pulled up into the line of skirmishers, his Spencer carbine at his shoulder.

He looked at Sergeant Troob. The sergeant shrugged and pointed to the colonel.

"Fire on my command!" Colt bellowed. The Indians continued their mounted charge forward. Colt could see a few rifles, but

11

mostly they carried lances and bows and arrows. When they hit the 100 yard mark Colt brayed the fire command, and nearly 50 carbines barked in a ragged barrage. Ten of the charging Indians slumped over and fell out of the charge. Two horses went down with head hits.

The rest of the Indians surged closer as the troopers with the Sharps pushed in a new round and the Spencer equipped men worked the trigger guard, pumping the old round out and a new one into place and fired. The average shooter with a Spencer could blast out the eight rounds in eight seconds, sending a surprising amount of lead at an enemy.

Most Indians had never stormed into a troop even half equipped with Spencer repeaters. The charge broke and swung to the left as the blue shirted men kept firing.

"Cease fire," Colt called, and the shooting stuttered down to silence. The Indians had turned down the valley.

Colt saw the chance to give chase and ordered the men to charge the savages. He spurred his mount forward and gave the cry as no bugler was present.

"Charge, fire at will!"

The men of C Troop pounded down the slight incline after the Indians. A dozen shots shattered the silence, then more carbines peppered the retreating Indians with hot lead as they soon turned and vanished into the fir cover on the far side of the valley.

Colt pulled his men up 200 yards from the cover and then told the sergeant to move them down the valley in a double rank so they could break into a battle formation quicker if needed. He looked around for Lieutenant Strachey. His carbine was still in the retaining ring on his saddle. He still held his reins with his right hand as he rode at a smart canter toward the other men forming into a column.

Colt went out to meet the officer but he passed Colt without a word or a glance. Colt turned and rode up and caught the horse's bridle and pulled it to a stop.

"Lieutenant Strachey, are you all right?"

The officer blinked for a moment, looked at the troop ahead of him, and then back up the valley where some of the wounded Indians were limping toward the cover of the trees.

"Yes. Yes, of course I'm all right. Why wouldn't I be? I'd say we won't be finding the hostiles today. They must be too far ahead of us."

"Lieutenant Strachey, didn't you hear the firing? We just engaged about 50 Cheyenne who came out of the woods."

"Impossible. I gave no order to fire. Impossible." He shook off the colonel's hand and rode down toward his troop, sitting erect in the McClellan saddle, his left hand holding the reins as he worked down to his men.

As the two officers rode up to the C Troop, now set up in a column of two's, Sergeant Troob came up to them and saluted.

Colt returned the salute but Lieutenant Strachey did not.

"Sir, a casualty report. We suffered two minor bullet wounds, a leg and an arm. One horse was hit badly and may not make it back to the fort. Otherwise we're ready for another engagement, if required."

Colt looked at Lieutenant Strachey. The man did not acknowledge the sergeant.

"Thank you, Sergeant Troob. Let's move the men out toward the fort. We've done all the good we're going to here. The rest of the hostiles are miles away by now. We don't have the supplies for a long chase."

"Yes, sir." Sergeant Troob saluted and swung his mount around. Colt waited until the sergeant was well out of hearing distance, then he moved over closer to the other officer. Colt slapped him hard on the side of the face. Lieutenant Strachey's head jolted to the side and his left hand came up to his face. He looked at Colt, then at the troop.

"Well. Seems like we've used up most of the day, Colonel. Afraid we won't be finding

14

the hostiles after all. I'd say it was time we headed back toward the fort. Can't find the bastards every time out, right Colonel?"

There was a twinkle in the lieutenant's eye as he kicked his horse into motion.

"That's the hell of this policy of reaction to an attack by the damned hostiles. They get to pick the time and the place and the number of men they'll have. We're at a disadvantage from the start. I tried to tell Colonel George Custer that when I served with him, but he ignored me."

Lieutenant Strachey laughed. "Hell, most of my superior officers have ignored me. Not a damn thing new about that, I'm afraid."

"Lieutenant!" Colt's voice cut through the air like a giant cleaver and snapped the officer's head around to look at his superior.

"Lieutenant Strachey, do you realize we were just attacked by a band of about fifty Cheyenne warriors using rifles and bows? Do you realize that you froze up solid, sat your horse like a statue and didn't snap out of it until the action was over and we were moving away from the scene?"

Strachey scowled and stared at Colt. "Sir, that is not something to joke about. I can assure you that I did not freeze up, that I was in complete control of myself at all times. . . ."

"Lieutenant! You froze. You didn't see the

15

hostiles attack us. You never looked in that direction, you failed to give any commands and your sergeant had to do it. We beat off the attack and the hostiles scattered into the woods. Now we're moving back toward the fort in a double file, *not in the usual four across formation.* Can you understand that, Lieutenant?"

"My God! Then it's true, you're not joking with me?"

"No jokes."

"My God! I must have blacked out. It could be that damn crack on the head I took in my quarters last night."

"Your whole troop could have been killed if it wasn't for the quick thinking of your First Sergeant. You and I are going to have a long talk as soon as we get back to the fort.

"I came on this patrol to get acquainted with the kind of problems we have up here, what's going on, and how my new men are reacting to the situation. I didn't expect to learn quite this much."

"Colonel, I've never had a black mark in my personal file. I'd hope we can keep this between ourselves."

Colt watched the man. He was not crawling or sniveling. But he was shaken. What was uppermost on Colt's mind was whether this had happened before and if so, under what circumstances.

"Lieutenant, you have two wounded men. This would be a good time for you to ride up and check on their condition." Colt stared hard at the man. The young officer took a deep breath, saluted smartly and rode up to the troops.

Colt took off his campaign hat and settled it slowly on his head. What in hell did he have here? The first thing he would do back at the fort would be to check over some personnel files, including that of Lieutenant Strachey and of First Sergeant Troob. When he first saw the name on the roster he felt a twinge of memory haunting him, but nothing came of it. Now he would find out.

The telegraph wire had reported a problem on the rail line that morning and soon a follow-up message from an operator on the site determined that the problem was Indian caused.

Such a situation triggered an immediate response by the army. Colt mounted up with C Troop as it headed up the rails of the Union Pacific railroad line to the northwest out of Larson City toward the town of Medicine Bow, another rail spawned settlement.

Twelve miles out of town they found the break in the rails with a work train already on hand repairing the damage. Colt and Lieutenant Strachey talked with the repair chief on the job.

"Looks to me like the heathens built a big fire on the tracks so they could burn the ties out." He pointed to a spot between the rails. "Here they must have dug out the road bed to get the ties to burn better. When the ties were burned through and the rails good and hot, they must have used their ponies and ropes and pulled the rails apart, bent the hell out of them."

The railroad track layer belched. "What the hell, now we got to replace two lengths of rails through here and put in about twenty new ties. Can't get done before the noon train is due through so they'll hold it at Larson City. Some of my boys said it looked like a whole passel of hoof prints pointing north right out there aways."

Lieutenant Strachey sent his scouts out to check and they came back a few minutes later.

"At least thirty sets of horse prints, sir," the corporal who led the two Indian scouts reported. "White Deer said they're moving north and in no rush."

So C Troop had followed the easy to read trail for ten miles. Then ahead they saw a lone Indian skyline himself on a ridge in the edge of the Larson mountain foothills.

"He wanted us to see him," Lieutenant Strachey said. "What in hell are they up to?"

The column rode for another two hours,

then they saw three scouts ahead of them.

"Back guards," the lieutenant said. "We must be catching up with them."

A half hour later they started up the small valley with the two wings of forest covered sides and Colt had smelled the hostiles.

Now, as the troop made its way back toward the fort, Colt knew that he had to find out for sure the whole story on First Lieutenant Rodney Strachey. Was the man fit to be a field officer in the United States Army and have 50 lives depending on him? That was the big question Colt had to get answered, and get it done quickly.

CHAPTER TWO

It was well after dark when the riders from C Troop arrived back at the fort. Colt remembered one Eastern woman thinking that every Western army fort had a wall and a high stockade around it with gates and tight security.

Very few such secure forts were ever built by the army after the Civil War, and those only in specifically difficult situations. Fort Phil Kearny up on the Bozeman trail in Wyoming was the only one Colt could think of, and it was abandoned in '68. The Indians promptly burned it to the ground.

Colt turned his horse over to his orderly who took her to the paddock and rubbed her down. He hurried into his office and wondered where the personnel files were.

Major Whit Longley sat in his office waiting for the Commander.

"How'd it go?"

"Damn poorly." He looked around the office but no one else was there. "What do you know about Lieutenant Strachey?"

Major Longley shrugged. He was a lean man, would be what a rancher would call a "poor feeder" in a fattening pen. He couldn't put on a pound if he tried. He was 43 years old, about five-six, weathered, wrinkled, smoked a pipe constantly, unmarried and had a hankering for strong drink which he kept under strict control. He sucked on his pipe, palmed it and looked up at his Commander.

"Enough to know you'll be interested in his file." He picked it up from his desk and handed it to the Colonel. "Figured you might want to check out one certain Sergeant Troob as well. You must have met him today."

"You know a lot about these men I don't," Colt said.

"Won't take you long."

Colt opened the file on First Lieutenant Rodney Strachey. There were the usual letters, memos, change of assignment record. Schooling: West Point three years ago, last post, and then his orders to come here.

Colt looked up. "I don't understand."

"You're right, Colonel, I figured the same thing, but I just let it ride because there was no reason to question it. He's been here about six months now."

"But there's not a blemish, not a black eye. Not one single drunken brawl or letter of rep-

21

rimand. There never has been a First Lieutenant in this man's army with such a clean sheet."

Whit Longley grinned. "I know, I checked through your file when it came in a week before you got here."

They laughed. "That's what I mean. If you're human you mess up somewhere along the line."

"So what are you saying, Colonel?"

"Somebody cleaned his file, put it through the wash, kept it all pretty and white."

"What does that mean?"

Colt sat down. "Pour me a shot of that rye whiskey you've got in your bottom drawer. You don't need to have one. I like to drink alone."

Whit grinned. "I see you've read my file, too."

"Always pays to know who's on the team."

Whit poured two fingers of rye in a water glass and handed it to Colt. Whit looked at the bottle for several seconds, then pushed the cork in the top and put the whiskey back in his bottom drawer.

Colt sipped the liquor and rubbed his jaw. "What does a clean record mean? Either the man is masquerading in his real role of the second coming of Christ, or the file was cleaned of everything to hide something big.

Right off, it was a dumb idea to make it so clean. Which leads me to think that the man in question probably did the laundry work himself on the papers."

"Damn, but we've got a pair of brilliant minds working on this together. My suspicions, exactly."

Colt sipped the last of the rye and put the glass down. "He was stationed last at Fort McPherson over in Nebraska. Let's make a gentle inquiry to see what we can find out. Send out a confidential dispatch on the train to the Fort Commander there asking for a quick report on the young man, any unusual behavior, any questionable activities, anything that he might have pulled out of his file. Mention that his file is simply too clean to be believed."

"Right, Colonel, I'll get at it first thing in the morning and have it off on the noon train eastbound." Whit hesitated. "You want to look at this other file, Colonel?"

"Sergeant Troob?" Colt shook his head. "I've had enough surprises for one night. Put it on my desk and I'll take a look in the morning." He checked his pocket watch. "It's after nine o'clock? Damn! I'll get skinned alive when I get home, even if it is just next door." Colt rubbed his forehead. "Don't even remember if the troops had supper. Guess we didn't. Might be something left if I move out." He waved at Whit and walked outside and next door to the Fort Commander's quarters.

He slipped in the door and saw Doris sitting in the rocker near the big lamp reading. She smiled, looked up and stood at once.

"I've got some supper warming in the oven."

Colt watched her, so pretty in the lamplight. For a moment he thought of her the way he first saw her in a squaw dress, with her hair in a braid, her face dirty and fear freezing her as she saw him in the Comanche tipi with his bloody knife. The next minute he told her who he was and they gathered up Sadie and little Dan and slipped out of the shelter and hurried to the horses.

Now she had her long black hair tied up in a bun at the back of her neck as she went to the stove and took out a supper fixed hours before.

"The mashed potatoes are wilted, but with enough gravy they should be fine. Pork chops! They came in on the train this morning and I got some from Hank's, that butcher shop in town. They bring them packed in ice from Omaha I've heard."

He sat down and she served him, then sat across the small table and watched him eat.

"I was thinking about White Eagle today. I don't know why. He really tried to help his people." She looked at Colt, her soft brown eyes sad. She reached out and touched Colt's arm. "It's a collision of two cultures. They both can't occupy the same place at the same time."

Colt nodded, wondering what had spawned this line of thinking all of a sudden.

"I mean, the Comanche, and I guess all of the plains tribes, are really warrior societies. The boys from Danny's age are taught to be warriors, how to fight and ride, and raid and kill. I didn't pay so much attention to it then, but now that I remember — oh, it's just . . . just terrible."

"I agree. But we're certainly not going to give in and let the hostiles run wild through our settlements."

"Oh no, we can't do that. So the answer is the reservation. Lock them up in a piece of ground where they can play at their games of war with each other, but not the white man."

"It's worked in places, with many of the eastern tribes. It will work here, if we do it right."

Doris shook her head. "I didn't mean to get so serious, it just sort of bubbled over," she brightened. "You should have seen what Danny did today."

Before she could tell him, Colt found himself talking to her about Lieutenant Strachey. When he finished all the way to the clean personnel file, he shook his head.

"I just can't figure it out."

"He's been on three different army posts in the last three years? Isn't that unusual? You've often said that on many of the posts soldiers assigned there when the fort is built, often serve out their enlistment there and maybe stay right there to retirement. Why had this officer moved around so much? Or has he been transferred, *not at his request.*"

Colt finished the second pork chop and laughed softly. "Woman, you are really getting to be army. That's an army phrase, and you know what it means. Yes, he's hiding something, but why wasn't it in his file?" He finished the potatoes and gravy and then put some plum jam on a slab of home made bread and took a bite.

"Was he transferred to give him a second chance? To let him start with a clean slate? The more I think about what happened today, the worse it gets. He could have led fifty men into a slaughter up there. Sergeant Troob practically took over command. He would have had to if I hadn't been there, I'm sure of that. He wouldn't have let the men be chopped up.

"Strachey . . . we'll see what happens in a few days. A dispatch would get from here to the middle of Nebraska in one day at least. Maybe in three days, we'll know."

He stood, bent and kissed Doris on the neck. "You stay right there. I'm going to tuck the kids in and let them know they still have a daddy. Then I'm coming back and see if I can persuade you to make me feel like a really married man."

She kissed him back and smiled. "Colonel, sir, no real persuasion is going to be needed. Let me wash these dishes first and by then I'll be suggesting something myself — in the bedroom."

The next morning, Colt got to his desk before breakfast and read the file on Sergeant Troob. It was all there: the training, the service, the awards, the commendations, even a Certificate of Merit medal along with the circumstances.

The medal was awarded for distinguished service involving peril of life and was never given without some outstanding effort. Colt never got one. As he read, everything became much clearer.

Sergeant Troob had fought in the Civil War. He had been a full colonel in command of a regiment and served under General

Sheridan. He was wounded twice, and was in line to move up to his first star when the war ended.

His permanent rank was First Lieutenant. After the war the army was cut down from 2.2 million men to a little more than 25,000. He was told he could remain in the army but would have to take a temporary reduction in rank to Second Lieutenant, and that there would be little chance for advancement for several years.

He had taken a discharge instead, stayed out of the army for a year and then enlisted as a private. Two years later he was a sergeant and after another year a First Sergeant. He was such a good soldier he couldn't be kept down. But now he was frozen in rank again.

Colt put the file down and nodded. No wonder he had been so ready to take command. He was ten times the field officer that Lieutenant Strachey was. The man must have tremendous will power and confidence to be able to serve under men like Strachey. Colt didn't think he'd have the guts or the patience to do it.

He went back to his quarters and ate four eggs for breakfast and a big bowl of hot oatmeal and brown sugar.

"Now I'm ready to tackle another day," Colt said, kissing Doris and swinging Sadie and Danny around in the living room.

"When can we go on a picnic?" Sadie asked. Colt brushed long blonde curls out of her eyes and kissed her cheek again. He remembered how she looked when he rescued her from the Comanches almost two years ago.

"Tomorrow. Tomorrow for sure we'll go on a picnic. You tell your mother." He returned the salute from Danny and slipped out the front door.

Colt stopped outside the door of the commander's quarters, and looked around the fort. It was like most army installations, built roughly around a parade ground a little over 100 yards square. The buildings were of sawed lumber.

On the left side of the square sat officers' quarters and the fort headquarter's office. The commander's quarters were next door and the adjutant's rooms next to that. In a row behind the officer country were three large buildings that housed visitors and guest quarters, then the ordnance shops and weapons rooms and the fort magazine. Toward the outside of the square was the bachelor officers' mess and the sutler's store. On the top of the square were positioned the married and bachelor officer quarters.

The telegraph line from the main Union

Pacific lines ran between the sutler's store and the married officers' quarters and ended at the fort headquarters. An operator was on duty in the small telegraph office 24 hours a day.

Right now there were 27 officers on post and 14 of those were married with families on post. On the right hand side of the square were the stables, tack room, farrier and smithy, with the paddock for some 400 horses surrounded by a sturdy six strand barb wire fence to hold the animals and give them ten acres to graze.

Below the smithy on the far side were 18 married enlisted men's quarters, and 17 were full. The barracks for the 400 enlisted men completed the fort's complement.

At the bottom of the square sat the guard house, the enlisted men's company kitchens and mess hall. Filling out the bottom of the quad was the large quartermaster warehouse and storage rooms.

It was a neatly laid out post, well constructed, and should last for as long as the army had need for protecting the railroad and the settlers who were beginning to move into this Cheyenne and Arapaho hunting ground.

Colt well expected that the Indians would give trouble for years, until the last bands were talked into heading for the reservations and put their war paint away. That might take a long time and a lot of U.S. Army red blood before it was accomplished.

Colt walked on to his office, pushed open the door and found Major Longley already at work.

"Morning," he said and poured a cup of coffee for his superior officer. "I roughed out a dispatch to the Commander at Fort McPherson and put it on your desk. I let them know we were curious about the man without sounding like there was any serious problem."

"Good, I'll look it over." Colt nodded at the closed door to the telegraph room. "Anything on the wire for us overnight?"

"Not a whisper."

"Good. Oh, I went through Troob's background this morning. No wonder he had no problem taking over a company. The man deserves much better than he has now. What's the status on field commissions?"

"About the same. Almost impossible to get one approved except in remarkable circumstances."

"Troob served under General Sheridan."

"I see your point. It's something to consider. You know the basic reason for a field commission is need. There must be a pressing and urgent need for the rank 'in order to protect the men of the command, or to expedite the mission of the unit so involved.' "

"Sounds familiar."

"You want to pull Lieutenant Strachey off duty?"

Sergeant Johnny McIntyre, the post First Sergeant, came in with dispatches from the morning train that went through westbound at six A.M.

"Good morning, sirs," McIntyre said to his Commanders, then went to his desk and began sorting through the dispatches. Colt waved his adjutant into his private office and closed the door.

"No, we won't pull Strachey. I told him I wanted to have a long talk with him, so I've got to do that before we learn anything from his previous post. I'll keep it easy but pointed and hope that he'll straighten out. If he has some physical problem, I'm not afraid to let him out on my patrol as long as Colonel Troob is with him."

"We shouldn't get into the habit. . . ."

"Yes, sorry. I'm getting mad at the army about that. He should have his own company, at least. He's probably never asked for a commission again, but damnit, it's about time."

CHAPTER THREE

J. Thorndike Dobson waited on the last customer and closed the front door of the Marshall's Emporium slightly after six-fifteen that evening in Larson City.

"We never lock the front door as long as a clerk is in the store," the owner, Clay Marshall, had told Dobson a thousand times. "If we're in the store, it's open," was another favorite of the old skinflint who owned the town's biggest store, right in the center of Larson City at First Street and Main.

J. Thorndike had been a clerk in the store for four years now. He was saving up his money and learning as much as he could about running a general store. His most treasured dream was to move on west and open up a store of his own. It would be the Dobson Emporium and General Merchandiser. He liked the sound of it, and knew it would take a double sign for the front of the store. He could open his store somewhere in Idaho, he hoped, or maybe even Washington Territory.

He had the ten thousand dollars inheritance in the St. Louis bank drawing interest, but it would take more than that to start a big store. Maybe he would at last decide to start small and grow larger with time and lots of work.

J. Thorndike was a bachelor at 26, with a balding head of brown hair, wore spectacles for reading and favored suspenders over a belt. His jaw jutted forward from a mouth of good teeth, but his nose had a habit of running, and he didn't know what caused it. He used two handkerchiefs a day, and no medication seemed to stop it. His slate gray eyes were without humor and his nose had a slight crook in it from being pounded and pushed around in school in St. Louis.

He was a fastidious man, well groomed, well dressed, and hated things out of their place. That's what made him such a good storeman. He could find anything in the store because he placed it in a particular and logical location.

He lived in a room over the storeroom that he built himself. He told Mr. Marshall he would work for five dollars a month less if he could stay in the store. That way he could save four to six dollars a month in room and board. Every penny counted to J. Thorndike.

He had never been comfortable around

women, and had not sown his wild oats as many young men do. In fact, J. Thorndike was still a virgin. He had thought about trying out one of the fancy ladies down at the Star and Garter Gaming House, but never quite got up enough nerve.

Next to his passion for retailing, J. Thorndike threw himself into the Save the American Indian Foundation. It was a charitable organization in Chicago that sent out lecturers and wrote tracts and pamphlets describing the dire situation of the American Indian, and showing how countless tribes from the eastern states had already been nearly wiped out by civilization and the treatment of them by the hostile and uncaring U.S. government.

J. Thorndike talked about the plight of the American Indian whenever he could. In his free time he went door to door asking for donations to the foundation. He was rewarded for his efforts with many insults and caustic comments, and indeed was bodily thrown out of one house. He decided it was his cross to bear and he would do so bravely. What little cash he was given was sent quickly to Chicago and he received more literature, glowing letters of progress, and a personal note urging him to canvass his town again for the much needed donations.

Now as he sat in his small room in the second floor of the storeroom, he thought about his quest. There had been a new commander named at Fort Larson, less than a quarter of a mile north of the small town. Dobson would visit him this Sunday and express his outrage at the army's butchering of the native Americans.

Yes, in two days it would be Sunday. After services he would take his horse and ride out to the fort and ask, no, demand, to see the Commanding Officer. That fool, Major Longley would probably still be there, but J. Thorndike could weather his scorn. He had to see the top officer at the fort.

Perhaps somehow he could influence the new commander. Perhaps somehow he could make him see that these were human beings that they were slaughtering. How would the Commander react if the reverse were true and the Indians raided the fort and killed his wife and children? Of course he would have to learn if the new commander had a family.

Yes, he would do it. Sunday for sure. He checked his watch. It was time. Friday night was meeting night. They would gather tonight in Priscilla Hilferty's house. The Widow Hilferty was well fixed, and she had given most of the donations which he had sent to Chicago. She was a good friend. He knew people around town had joked about them, the perfect match of oddballs, some had said.

J. Thorndike was troubled by that because Priscilla was a nice woman, not young any more at 32, but he had felt that she was attracted to him. Well, that would have to wait. He had no time for ladies right now.

Ten minutes later he stepped on the Hilferty porch and lifted the knocker. The door opened and Priscilla swung it wide as she smiled at him. She was tiny, almost birdlike, with small sharp features, wire rimmed spectacles and prematurely gray hair in a bun on top of her head. She wore a white lace dress buttoned to her chin and wrists and sweeping the floor.

"J. Thorndike, so good of you to come. Amelia is already here. Reverend Wilbur will be here directly. He's making a sick call."

Priscilla took his arm and walked him into the parlor. The room was furnished as if it were a Boston sitting room. A carpet on the floor came almost to the walls. Polished cherry wood chairs with soft cushions on them sat around the room. Fancy cross stitched slogans in frames decorated one wall. The wallpaper was a bright spring theme of pinks and greens. A long settee upholstered in a late eastern fashion with two chairs to match were the centerpiece of the room.

Priscilla sat on the long couch and pulled J. Thorndike down beside her.

"So nice you could come, Amelia," J. Thorndike said, nodding to the rather stern faced woman in one of the soft chairs. She was in her forties, married, and wore black a year after her latest child died at birth. She spoke to no one she didn't have to and now simply nodded. Her husband was the undertaker for the town of Larson City.

Priscilla sat close to J. Thorndike and kept holding his arm. He cleared his throat and moved slightly away from her and she let go of him.

"Well, since three of us are here, we should begin. It is the appointed time. So, what do you have to report Amelia, on the situation of the closest Indians, the Cheyenne?"

Amelia smiled and shook her head. "I asked everybody I knew in town, but there just isn't much information on the Cheyenne. They are a warrior tribe, they live by hunting and gathering fruits and nuts that grow wild. They know nothing of agriculture, and are constantly moving. The buffalo continue to be the staple of their diet and furnishes their utensils, food supply, bowstrings, tipi covering, robes for winter . . . almost everything they need. When the buffalo are gone, the Cheyenne will be hard put to survive."

"But how can we stop the hide men from killing the buffalo?" J. Thorndike asked. "Actually we're too late already. The big kills took place over the past six to eight years. Most buff hunters I hear about say the buffs will be nearly extinct in ten more years."

Reverend Wilbur had come in the open door and now slipped into a chair near Amelia.

"Sorry," he said. He was an average sized man, a little heavy, wore no wedding ring and had a nervous habit of clearing his throat every minute or so. He wore a dark blue suit and white shirt with a reverse collar above his dark vest.

"Dreadful news," the preacher said. "I hear the new Fort Commander is a man with a long background of killing Indians. In Texas he was known as Two Gun, and then he brutalized Indians in Kansas and down in the Washita Valley. Just dreadful. I'm afraid we will have a real problem on our hands here."

"What can we do about it?" J. Thorndike asked. "We must do more than just meet and wring our hands. We must take action, even if that action could be outside the law. Someone must stand up and be counted. Just the same way that Christ drove the legal money changers from the temple."

"Amen," Preacher Wilbur said. "Of course

39

. . . I must remember my position. I can't do anything that would bring discredit upon the church, but I'll stand with you whenever possible."

"So, some ideas, people," J. Thorndike asked. "What can we do to bring this Indian butcherer up on his heels?"

"First we must talk," Amelia said. "We need to go out to the fort and protest."

"I plan on doing that first thing Sunday afternoon," J. Thorndike said. "That part is taken care of. What else can we do?"

J. Thorndike settled down. He knew that they would talk and plan and argue for two hours. Eventually, if anything was done, it would be up to him to do it. Why couldn't he attract some people to this group with ability and some willpower?

An hour later Priscilla brought in tea and cookies, and they kept talking. They could picket the fort, they could send a telegram to the United States President and to the territorial governor. They could insist that the county sheriff tell the army that any Indian activity inside the county was the sheriff's responsibility and the army must keep hands off.

Twenty minutes after the cookies, Reverend Wilbur rose to leave, saying he had to sit in on the last of a deacons meeting. Ten min-

40

utes later Amelia decided she had better walk home before it got dark.

Priscilla motioned for J. Thorndike to stay as Priscilla left. When she came back, she smiled at him and crooked her finger.

"J. Thorndike, there's a small problem in the other room I wonder if you could help me with? You're so handy around the house and all."

"Yes, of course, Mrs. Hilferty. What seems to be the trouble?"

She led him across the room, down a short hall, and stepped into the bedroom. It was light enough inside to see. She had brought no lamp.

"The problem, Mrs. Hilferty?" J. Thorndike asked, not really understanding.

She was facing the window and her hands were busy for a moment. Then she turned around and the front of her dress was open. Her chemise had been pulled up to show both of her bare breasts.

Priscilla caught his hands and held him.

"J. Thorndike, my problem is right here. I'm a woman without a man and I need one just ever so bad. I know you're not forward, and I want you so much. Don't I appeal to you as a woman, even a little?"

She lifted his hands, placed them over her breasts and reached her arms around him.

41

She hugged him and kissed his cheek and looked up at him.

J. Thorndike had never touched a woman's breast before. He was aware of his hips jerking and then he and the woman slid sideways onto the bed. When they fell, she came on top of him and somehow one of her breasts was near his face. He stared at it a moment, then looked up at Priscilla.

She smiled. "Just do anything you want to, sweetheart," she said.

J. Thorndike sighed and opened his mouth. It was about time, he decided. Yes, it was about time.

Priscilla sighed and then trembled. "Yes, J. Thorndike, yes! We'll worry about the Indians, tomorrow."

CHAPTER FOUR

The party had been planned for Saturday night. Ordinarily, it would be the adjutant's wife's duty to throw the welcome party for the new Fort Commander, but there was no Mrs. Longley, so the task fell to the next senior officer's wife, Nina Vining, wife of Captain Ormsby Vining, the quartermaster.

Colt knew it was coming, and was told two days ago about it. Doris had been delighted and made a new dress for herself for the occasion. She actually tore three dresses apart and fit and pieced them back together into one that was flashy and different. She was excited.

Colt spent the morning talking to Lt. Strachey. It began on a sour note. There had not been anything in the dispatches from Fort McPherson about the request for information on the officer.

Strachey came into the Commander's office, and stood rigidly at attention, his campaign hat under his arm. When Colt looked up the officer saluted, and Colt returned the formality even though saluting was not required indoors.

"First Lieutenant Rodney Strachey reporting to the Commanding Officer as ordered, sir!"

"At ease, Strachey. Sit down. I'm trying to talk to as many of my key officers as possible so I can get a feel for the command and the people. Just like you do when you take over a new company."

Strachey sat in the chair across the desk but Colt noticed he sat on the very front edge of it, his back ramrod straight, and he was as tight as a Cheyenne war drumhead.

"Relax, Strachey. I understand you are West Point, class of sixty-five. That means you had no Civil War service."

"Just a bit, sir. We were graduated two months early and I was at Appomattox Court House on April 9 for Lee's surrender. However, I did fire a few shots in anger the preceding week."

"I see. How did you react to the fighting?"

"It wasn't what I expected. All of our four years of theory and tactics became background. Now I was in a specific situation and I had to fight and live or die in that bit of foggy real estate. It was eye opening, to say the least."

"Since then you've had three or four duty

assignments. Isn't this unusual?"

"Yes sir. I was simply in the wrong place. One fort was closed and I was reassigned. In another, a new commander came in and brought twelve officers with him, so the lowest twelve ranks were shipped out."

"Yes, fortunes of the army," Colt said. He stood and looked out the window at a cavalry troop drilling on the parade ground.

"You realize that I was not pleased with your performance on that patrol yesterday."

"Yes, sir. I blacked out. It was that crack on the head in my quarters. I went to the doctor and he said there was no concussion or other damage, so I should be fine now."

"Did the doctor tell you that the blackout could happen that long after the blow to the head?"

"He said he'd heard of it happening."

"Fine. Are you happy with your troop?"

"Yes, sir. Sergeant Troob is an experienced man who takes a lot of the load on himself."

"I'm going to leave you with the troop, Lieutenant. I just hope there are no more problems such as we had before."

"I'm all well now, sir. I promise that I'll be in top form."

"Oh, concerning West Point, I'm always interested in the class position a man graduates in from West Point. Just for the files, what was your graduating number?"

"I was sixteenth, sir, out of a class of fifty-four."

"Very good. You've heard of Colonel George Armstrong Custer, I would assume?"

"Yes sir."

"Did you realize that on July of 1862 he was a First Lieutenant? Exactly one year later, on July of 1863, he was promoted to Brigadier General of volunteers and was given command of a brigade of cavalry? He was only twenty-three years old. He was a Major General when he was twenty-five years old and commanded a division."

"No, sir. I wasn't aware that he was promoted so quickly."

"Custer graduated from West Point in a class of thirty-four. Do you know what position he held?"

"First, sir? The top slot?"

"No, he barely made it through and graduated thirty-fourth, dead last in his class."

"My God!"

"Remember, Lieutenant, position isn't everything. That will be all."

Lieutenant Strachey saluted, did a smart about face and left the room.

A few moments later, Major Longley knocked and came in the door.

"So, what do you think about Strachey?"

"I don't know. He's certainly intelligent enough to do the job, he's had the training at the Point. He's been promoted by someone in three years. But there's something that just rubs my fur the wrong direction."

"Mmmmmm. Felt the same way for the past three or four months." Major Longley took a heavy envelope from under his arm. "Maybe this will help. A dispatch that the railroad misplaced for a few hours. It came in on the morning train but got lost. They sent it out by messenger with an apology. It's the material from Fort McPherson."

Colt grabbed the envelope and tore it open. He shook out a sheaf of sheets bound together and two or three handwritten pages.

The letter was from a Major Zimmerman, adjutant at Fort McPherson. Colt read it.

"So you're the lucky post that drew Strachey. We really didn't know what to do with him when he was here for six months. Let me start at the beginning. The man has connections. He has an uncle in Washington D.C. who is a U.S. Senator. There should have been a letter in his file.

"I got so interested in the case that I made a hand copy of each item in the officer's permanent file for my own reference. I have known files such as his to be doctored along the line. It looks like his has been before it got to you.

"I'll send the whole file I copied, including orders, reprimands, court martials, his evaluation reports, and a letter from the Senator *demanding special attention* for this young Second Lieutenant. A real mess.

"Hope you can handle the situation. We promoted him so he was over-rank in his position here and then could get him transferred into a *need* situation there at Larson. Sorry."

Colt handed the letter to Whit and looked at the other documents. There had been one court martial where he was charged with dereliction of duty on a patrol, but he beat the accusation made by two enlisted men. The EM said the lieutenant had shrunk from his command responsibilities and only the action of two sergeants in the troop saved them from being wiped out by a band of hostiles.

Now Colt found the items he might expect to find in any file, small problems, an argument with an enlisted, a confrontation with a captain about Strachey being too familiar with his daughter at a dance, and the letter from the Senator on his Washington D.C. stationery directing the Fort Commander to promote Strachey the moment his two years duty were up, or the fort would be investigated by an Inspector General for mismanagement and below par operation.

Colt looked over the material quickly and handed it to Whit. He called in Sergeant McIntyre.

"Send someone to get Sergeant Troob. I'd like to talk to him as soon as possible."

"Yes, sir."

The sergeant left the room and Whit looked up. "We were right about there being a little bit of dirt in the man's background. You going to dump him?"

"Not yet. He'll get another chance. I just want to be sure I don't endanger the men of C Troop in the process."

Sergeant Troob reported to the Colonel less than seven minutes later. He wasn't even out of breath. Whit looked up when the sergeant came in and Colt nodded. The adjutant left the room taking the papers with him.

"Whit, nobody sees those but you and I. I want them sealed and in my desk when you're through."

The door closed and Colt turned to the sergeant.

"First Sergeant Troob, I have a copy of your army records, all of your records. You are a remarkable man."

49

"Beg pardon, Colonel, I'm just another soldier doing my job."

"I've been thinking about that patrol I went on with you. What are the men saying about their Troop Commander?"

"Not much, sir."

"How do they feel about what he did?"

"Most of them were too busy with the Cheyenne to notice, sir."

"But some did. You did. What did you think about his actions?"

"Not my place to comment on a superior officer's actions, Colonel."

"Colonel Troob, he's not your superior officer in fact, only in your current rank. Forget rank and rate and army. What is your opinion of the man and what he did?"

First Sergeant Troob took a deep breath. He had been standing at attention.

"Sergeant, at ease, please sit down."

He did.

Sergeant Troob looked at Colt for a moment. "Sir, I've seen two other men do what he did in heavy action in the Civil War. They were in over their heads. They had been trained to lead men, but had not been trained to watch men being blown apart in front of their faces. They had not been prepared to wipe their best friend's brains off their uniform and continue an attack.

"Lieutenant Strachey simply froze and shut off his mind. The danger, the death potential, the absolute horror of it became too much for his mind to accept, so he didn't participate."

"He said he blacked out from a blow on the head the day before," Colt said.

"That's horse piss, sir."

"Agreed." Colt stood and walked to the window, then to the door. He moved to a wall map showing 50 square miles of Wyoming in the southwest corner of the territory.

"Troob, what I have to figure out now is, will it happen again? Will he cave in like a foundering horse and endanger the lives of his troop?"

"Absolutely. It just depends on how tough the action is he's involved in."

"Your recommendation?"

"Sir, as an enlisted man, I can't make suggestions to a light colonel."

"Horse piss, Troob. Don't you freeze up on me and stop participating. You're too good a soldier to do that."

"Sir, the two men in my command who acted in a similar manner were a sergeant and a captain. As soon as I had the report I pulled them off line and sent them to the rear for an immediate discharge for mental/medical reasons. I never saw the two again."

Colt nodded. It was about what he had expected.

"I would like to do the same, but I need him in that slot. We're two officers short as it is. Also, if I didn't have you right beside him, I'd dump him in a minute. With you there we have insurance. I'm giving you an extended order, Sergeant. If, at any time in the future, Lieutenant Strachey exhibits the same or similar behavior as he did on the last patrol, you are to assume command at once, move the Lieutenant into a safe position, and use your judgment and training in continuing the action, or breaking off and returning the troop to the fort."

Colt watched the sergeant. "Can you accept that order, Troob?"

"Yes, sir. Because I have the feeling that Lieutenant Strachey will not willingly take another patrol into combat. He will be extremely careful about facing another situation where he thinks he might fail again."

"I agree. But there may come a time when I'll have to send C Troop into contact with the hostiles. If you have the slightest doubt that he's unable to command, assume command yourself. Now, the next topic. As soon as I can write up the paper work, I'm putting you up for a field commission."

Sergeant Troob shook his head.

"There hasn't been one granted since the Civil War, Sir."

"This is a *need* situation, you're qualified, you're West Point and a former light colonel with plenty of battle experience. Besides, I think I can get it into the hands of a friend of yours, General Sheridan."

"Phil Sheridan? He's still the commander of the Military Division of the Missouri, isn't he?" Troob shook his head. "Still, it will never go through."

"Damnit, it should! The army should never have lost you. I'm gonna give it my best shot and we'll see what happens."

Troob stood and saluted. "Thank you, sir."

Colt returned the salute. "Watch out for our problem. I'm glad you're here."

Colt watched the man walk out the door. Then he called in First Sergeant McIntyre who started digging into the regulations to find out what kind of a form was needed for a request for an emergency field commission.

CHAPTER FIVE

The welcome party that night was held in Major Longley's quarters. Four officers' wives had been there most of the day getting it ready, decorating, rolling up one rug so there could be dancing, getting the three musicians, a fiddle player, an accordian player and a guitar rehearsed and ready.

More women had spent the day baking and cooking so there would be a fancy dinner with more food than they had seen in weeks. A special order had been put in and was sent out from Omaha on the train.

Colt fussed as Doris straightened his dress uniform. He wasn't even sure it was up to date. They were changing regulations and uniforms so fast he couldn't keep up. At least as a light colonel he could wear whatever he wanted to until he met someone of higher rank.

He absolutely refused to wear the Prussian style dress helmet with the tassels. He used instead a new campaign hat, but did put on his saber.

"A fancy party is about the only thing these damn sabers are good for," he groused. Doris kissed him on the cheek.

"Yes sir, Colonel, sir!" she said and saluted him with the worst example of a salute he had ever seen. He broke up laughing. For tonight he would forget about the mess with Lieutenant Strachey. He would enjoy himself, maybe get a little drunk, and he would make sure none of the young lieutenants danced more than once with his wife.

"Prettiest girl at the party," he said, looking at her. "Hey, did I ever tell you I'm glad you were in White Eagle's tipi that night I came charging in?"

Doris looked up for a moment and her eyes brimmed with tears of joy. Then she wiped them away and kissed her Colonel on the lips. It was soft and sweet and gave him another thousand thanks for rescuing her.

He looked at the bedroom door. "We better get down there. We're fashionably late now. Did the girl come to stay with the kids?"

"A half hour ago," Doris said, smiling.

"This is part of the army too, I guess. I've been to enough of these shindigs, but never one for me — for us. Let's go."

Everyone was there when they knocked on the door ten minutes after six. Things were low key, the way these welcomes usually went until the whiskey flowed too freely. Colt had told the ladies to keep the hard liquor to a minimum, and have lots of fruit juices and sarsaparilla and tea and coffee.

There was quickly a receiving line for them, with Major Longley leading the way. He saluted smartly, introduced himself to Colt who then introduced him to Doris who shook his hand. He then moved to the punch table and caught up a cup of sweet cider.

The 27 officers of the fort were all there. The Officer of the Day and Officer of the Guard quickly gave their apologies and reported back to their duty posts.

After the last Second Lieutenant went through the line, in strict accordance to rank with married rank first, the ladies called them all to the kitchen and parlor where they had set up tables to form one long U-shaped seating arrangement.

The food was outstanding. They had wild turkey, pheasant, quail and chicken for the main course, with half a dozen different fresh garden vegetables, mashed potatoes like white mountains and giblet gravy in a blend of the domestic and wild birds' juices that kept Colt asking for more.

Before the evening was over, he found out who made the gravy and wheedled from her exactly how she did it. He was determined to have more gravy like that from his own kitchen.

Colt began enjoying himself halfway through the supper. Soon the talk around the table turned to war stories, and Colt stood and raised his hand. Every officer quieted immediately and only two women chattered for a moment before they saw him.

"Gentlemen, let there be no talk of war, or war stories, or Indian fighting or even of the army tonight. Let's tell strange and funny stories, and amuse ourselves. For one night, let's forget about the tough, necessary job that we're doing."

He heard several amens from around the table and launched into a story about how he got into trouble once with a farmer over his cow and how the cow had somehow become supper for 45 men.

"Not an army story," Colt said quickly. "Actually it's a bovine tale, because she was the star of the show that night and the next morning and well into the noon time stop for chow." Everyone laughed and they began to take turns with wild memories, some funny, some not so funny, and one tragic.

When the tales were spun and everyone well fed, Mrs. Vining stood and waved them to silence.

"If you gentlemen would help remove the

chairs and tables, I'll bring in the orchestra and the dancing will begin. As you might have figured out, we will have dessert at the stroke of midnight."

Major Longley eased up beside Colt and touched his shoulder.

"You know if that field commission goes through, the man will have to be transferred."

"I thought of that," Colt said quietly. "I owe it to this man. I realize a former enlisted can't be put back into the same troop now as an officer. In this case that wouldn't be a problem, but some of the other officers here on post would be. Yes, if it goes through he'll be moved by Phil Sheridan where he can do the most good."

"It's a long shot chance of going through."

"I know. I've always bet on losers. Let's see how I do on this one. You got the papers off to Phil?"

"Yes, on the noon train with three copies. Never seen such a well worded recommendation in my life."

"Had to, he deserves it."

The dancing began then, with the Colonel and his lady taking the first dance. It was a slow waltz, thank God, Colt thought as he did the three step around the cleared living and dining room area. By then people were spilling into the kitchen and the two bedrooms, where the ladies had arranged chairs, and small tables with juices and drinks so everyone could have something handy.

Whit Longley stared at the whiskey bottles, but when his hand went out it was for another cup of hot cinnamon cider from one of the steaming, covered pots.

"Congratulations," Doris said as she steadied his hand as she poured from the cider pot.

"Figured me out?"

"My father had a problem for a time," Doris said. "You are doing what I'd call extremely well." She squeezed his hand and moved on to serve someone else at the table.

The dancing continued, the war stories surged back again, and groups and clusters of wives and officers developed. Colt didn't try to read anything into it. He would learn enough tomorrow in a talk with Whit Longley.

Dessert came at midnight — more than 20 different kinds of home made pies.

It was nearly one o'clock before Colt realized that as the honored guest, none of the other officers would leave before he did. He got the floor, stopped the musicians, made a small thank you and marched out the door with Doris.

In their own bedroom, she smiled at him. They had sent the girl home and kissed the kids goodnight even though they were sleeping. Now Doris watched her husband.

"The other wives are right. They say that Fort Larson has the most handsome Commanding Officer of any post in the army. I was quick to agree with them." He kissed her and dropped on the bed.

He wouldn't worry about the Strachey situation. Not until tomorrow.

Sunday afternoon, Colt was surprised when he had a visitor. There had been no drills scheduled for the day, and no patrols were out. Most forts took it slow and steady on Sunday. The perimeter guards, who kept a visual check on those about to enter or leave the Fort area, stopped the civilian just as he was passing the guard house.

A few minutes later the Corporal of the Guard knocked on the Officer of the Day's door and informed him that the Commander had a civilian visitor.

For ten minutes the O.D. had listened to the diatribe belched out by J. Thorndike Dobson.

"Mr. Dobson, I'm not sure if the Fort Commander can see you today. I'll ask him. However, I would advise you to temper your statements about the military's treatment of the Indians. Many of the men on this fort have had friends killed by the hostiles, me included. I don't take kindly to hearing civilians, safe in your towns, berating the army. We're the ones out there getting shot at, cut up and dying."

The Officer of the Day stared at Dobson for a moment, then went to the guard house door. "You sit right there until I get back."

Five minutes later, Colt stepped into his office and shortly thereafter the O.D. brought Dobson to the door.

"Sir, this civilian wants to have a word with you." The OD. stepped back and let Dobson inside, then closed the door and went back to his post.

Colt looked at Dobson. He had been briefed on who the man was by the O.D. who knew of him and his small group in town. Colt took out a pearl handled revolver and laid it on the desk. He looked up at Dobson.

"Yes, Mr. Dobson, you wanted to talk with me?"

Colt began to clean the weapon, breaking it down into its component parts and wiping off each one.

"Yes, Colonel. I understand you're now in command of the fort. I am here to launch an official protest of your treatment of the Indians by members of this post."

Colt looked up. "Mr. Dobson, you have personal knowledge of this treatment? You witnessed some outrage?"

"Well, no, not personally. But it's a well known fact. . . ."

Colt slammed his hand on the desk and stood.

"No! I will not listen to hearsay. I will not stand here and let some civilian slander the United States Army. Mr. Dobson, if and when you receive any first hand, personally observed evidence of United States Army misconduct, I'll be more than happy to hear you out, to take down your statement and make an official inquiry. Such inquiry will be passed along through army channels to the proper investigating body.

"Now, I repeat. Do you have any hard, legal evidence of any United States Army personnel mistreating, attacking, wounding or killing any Indian in my jurisdiction?"

"Well, no, not personally. However. . . ."

"Good day, Mr. Dobson. I don't have time to engage in talk with a man with no evidence. Get your evidence, write it down in sworn statements giving time, place, and names of those units involved and which Indian tribes and bands were involved. Then I'll be more than happy to talk with you."

"You are excused. Sergeant!"

Sergeant McIntyre opened the door. He had been called to his post by the O.D.

"This way, Mr. Dobson. I'll escort you off the post, for your own protection."

"But . . . but I didn't say what I came here to say."

"Evidence, Mr. Dobson, I can deal only with evidence. Thank you for stopping by."

J. Thorndike Dobson stammered twice, found he could not present anything of a substantial nature, and walked quickly out of the room with Sergeant McIntyre escorting him. The sergeant took him back to his horse and watched as the civilian angled toward town.

A hundred yards away, J. Thorndike stopped and looked back at the fort. This new commander was much more difficult to deal with than the former one. There would have to be some different tactics taken to gain his attention. Just what could those tactics be?

Letters to the Department of the Army and to the President would be essential. A letter to the Territorial Governor would be good. But more was needed. Much more.

The idea of marching in a protest parade in front of the fort came to mind. He had seen people marching back and forth, labor people he thought they were. They could do the same thing with signs about the army brutality, such as that at Sand Creek, the massacre of 300 or 400 Indians. Yes, now he had an idea to work with.

He rode slowly back toward town. He would go and tell Priscilla about his meeting. He wouldn't tell her exactly what happened. They could plan what to write on the signs they would carry.

J. Thorndike thought about Friday night in Priscilla's bedroom and he felt his cheeks grow warm. It had been an experience he would never forget. He hadn't stayed all night, but for three hours he had been moved and thrilled and delighted far beyond anything he had ever dreamed of before.

He shook his head to clear it. Enough of that. He had to think about the Indians. Someone had to stand up for them. Here it would be him and Priscilla, and Amelia, and maybe the preacher.

Yes, the four of them could march in front of the fort. The *Larson City Light* would run a story about them, maybe on the front page. He would talk to Edward about a story. Yes. Perhaps his visit today had not been wasted after all.

CHAPTER SIX

Brave Bull's first wife had selected the camp-site, as was her responsibility as the leader of the band's wife. It hugged a foot deep, 20 feet wide, tributary to the much larger Larson River that ran north out of the mountains until it turned east and finally emptied into the North Platte River.

Fifty tipis scattered along a quarter mile stretch of the stream on both sides in this favorite camping spot of many summers before. Brave Bull's band had been coming here for as long as most of them could remember.

They always left before the grass was killed by the horses, and before they harvested all of the nuts, berries and roots. They made sure they left enough so Mother Earth could replenish herself before their next visit.

Summer was the best time for the Cheyenne. They had found a small herd of buffalo and harvested enough animals to make two new tipi covers and to supply buffalo robes that were getting thin and wearing out. New gut for bowstrings was taken, as well as the 30 or 40 other parts of the big lumbering beasts that provided almost every item of clothing, shelter, and food that the Cheyenne needed.

Now it was time for war, for raiding and for stealing young women from other tribes to help build up the population of the Cheyenne.

Two Dogs' tipi sat near the water, but far enough back so there was a pleasant resting place in front of the ten pole shelter. Two Dogs had two wives and a slave, and would soon ride out to find another woman slave. A new slave was much easier to steal from another tribe than to pay ten or fifteen horses to buy another wife.

He sat in front of his tipi, near his shield and lance and bow. They were positioned just outside of the tent, ready to be grabbed as he charged to his war pony to defend the camp.

Two Dogs was pleased for the moment. His two wives and the slave worked scraping the hides of the two buffalo he had killed in the recent hunt. There was fresh meat for three days, and lots of jerky and soon pemmican for the winter.

He sighed. The slave was a continuing disappointment. Just after he captured her she had fought him every time he parted her legs. When she had some fight in her, he had enjoyed sharing her with some of his warrior friends.

But now she was ugly, dirty, passive. She hardly knew when he touched her. She wore rags even when he offered her better clothes such as a clean squaw dress and an old Pony Soldier shirt he had stripped off one of the army devils. At least she worked. If she did not work, she did not eat. He had told First Flower to be sure she worked, and his first wife had seen to it. The first month the slave had been whipped every day for not working. Now the sores were healed, but the fire had gone out of her eyes. She was like a whimpering, beaten dog. Only this slave woman did not whimper.

Sometimes he wondered what she thought, or if she had a mind left to think with. The White Eyes were not very smart sometimes. This might be one of the slow witted ones. Twice she had tried to escape. The second time he made her go about the camp naked, let the men call to her and grab her if they wanted to and throw her down in the middle of the camp.

She had never tried to run away again.

Two Dogs sighed. Perhaps he had treated her wrong. But if he had taken her into his tipi and cared for her like a third wife, surely the young woman would have been killed. First

Flower had so much as told Two Dogs this when he first brought the large, blonde woman to his tipi after the raid far to the east.

The slave had a good woman's body: fine breasts for suckling a child, good wide hips for an easy birth. She was big and strong, but she had never been with child. Almost a year now she had been slave to him.

He called her Lost Woman, and now she truly seemed lost. She had learned her new name quickly after many beatings, and now responded to it automatically.

"Lost Woman, come here." Two Dogs said the words lightly yet she heard him. She put down her stone scraper, left the unfinished hides and hurried toward where he sat.

First Flower looked up and scowled.

Two Dogs spat at her and she looked back down at her work.

Lost Woman stopped in front of her owner, then she knelt down so he could talk to her.

Two Dogs had not allowed her to speak English, so he had learned none from her. Now she could not teach him any. He should have learned. He would be a valuable man in the band if he could speak the devil soldier's tongue.

"Inside the tipi," he ordered her. She had learned certain important words, and responded to them. Now she ducked inside the

68

flap opening and stood waiting for him. He came in shortly, pulled apart the tattered squaw dress she wore and looked at her naked body. She was thin, but still she aroused him. He motioned for her to lie on the low bed built just off the floor as was the Cheyenne custom.

She did so and stared at the smoke hole above. She made no move to resist when Two Dogs stripped off his breechclout and mounted her.

When he was satisfied, Two Dogs rolled away from her, put on his breechclout and searched for something at one side of the tipi. Soon he came to her with a much worn squaw dress. At one time it had been adorned with beads and elk's teeth, but now it was plain.

It was far the best dress she had used in this tipi. He thrust it at her and left.

Lost Woman sat up slowly, lifted the dress on over her head but did not look at it. She hurried outside to the flat place where the new buffalo hides had been staked down to the ground. First Flower saw her coming and shrieked and ran at her, but Two Dogs snarled three words and his first wife stopped.

"She's wearing my dress!" First Flower screeched.

"I gave it to her," Two Dogs spat. "Even

my slaves must be dressed or I will lose favor with the council."

Lost Woman did not understand all of it. She continued to work the skin, knelt where she had been and began scraping with the sharp rock, working the flesh and tallow off so it would dry straight and flat and would be easy to cure in the sun.

Her arms ached from six hours of scraping already. She knew she would be there until there was not enough light to see to do the work.

It didn't matter. She would work until one day she died. It didn't matter. Months ago she had given up any hope of ever getting away. It was after the last time she tried to steal a horse and ride to freedom. She was a good rider, but they had caught her within two miles.

Two Dogs had been so angry he made her go around naked. For two weeks she had done her work with no clothes on. Several times a day one of the other warriors would see her and push her to the ground and take her wherever they were.

At first she had been so mortified she couldn't keep her eyes open. After the third or fourth day she never felt it. It was as if she had no more than said hello to someone.

Now, all she could do was work. She ate

whatever she could. First Flower let her eat little, hoping that she would die. First Flower was jealous of her and in every way made her life miserable.

Once Lost Woman had awakened inside the tipi last winter. Usually she had to sleep outside, but Two Dogs was afraid she would freeze to death that particularly cold night. Lost Woman had been brought in and told to sleep at the side of the tipi on the floor. She did so and woke up during the night.

Lost Woman had seen the skinning knife and had grabbed it and lifted it over sleeping First Flower, but no matter how much she hated the Indian woman, she could not kill her. She had put the knife down and gone back to her bed. It was only then that she had seen Two Dogs holding his throwing knife. If she had killed First Flower the warrior would have killed her.

Now Lost Woman brushed back some hair that fell in her eyes. It was starting to grow out again, but still it was no more than two inches long. First Flower had cut it off by the hand-fuls whenever Lost Woman did not do as she was supposed to. At last she had only a fringe of hair less than half an inch long all over her head.

First Flower had a child, nearly two years old. The little boy still nursed. Lost Woman learned that Indian women usually nursed their babies until they were five years old. A warrior could not have intercourse with his wife while she was nursing. No wonder the Indians had such a low birth rate. No wonder the warriors wanted more than one wife.

Lost Woman continued to scrape. First Flower shouted something at her and she understood only one word. "Fire." She got up and went to the tipi and made sure the small fire there was still burning. She built it up to the level that would produce good coals for cooking. She had just finished when First Flower came in the tipi flap.

She grunted when she saw the fire done just right. Tonight she was boiling up a rabbit stew. Two Dogs had brought back the big jack from his hunt early that morning. Two Dogs was a big eater. He insisted on as much food as possible, but it was his job to do the hunting. The women looked for roots and nuts and berries. The more they found, the more they could eat.

Lost Woman usually ate as many as she put in the clay pots, but she had to do it when First Flower was not looking.

That evening when the camp quieted, and Two Dogs took in the flap of his tent for the night, Lost Woman stretched out on the old buffalo robe she had found when the camp moved. She had claimed it as her own. First Flower had pulled it away from her and for the first time Lost Woman had screamed at the Indian woman. Two Dogs had laughed and awarded Lost Woman the robe as her own.

She chose a spot closer to the rushing water for her bed tonight, and now looked up at the summer stars through the light screen of leaves. This was the hardest part of the day for her. No work to keep her hands and her mind busy. Nothing to do but . . . think. She had decided months ago that if she tried to think she would drive herself crazy. There was no hope, she had no future, she had to make do the best she could, minute to minute. If she took care of the first minute that would lead to the second and then to the first hour and soon the whole day would be over. Cope, not hope, had to be her resolve.

The plan had worked for almost a year. It was summer again. She had been captured in summer. She had just finished the breakfast dishes and her husband and the farm hand had gone out to start repairing some fencing when the raiders hit. Thirty Cheyenne had swept down on the tiny farm, burned the house, slaughtered her husband and the farm hand as they tried to defend themselves with the shovels they carried.

Then the frightening confrontation with Two Dogs who had touched her and claimed her and tied her hands and feet as they looted the house and barn, rounded up the three horses and killed the only milk cow. They butchered her and took two quarters of the meat with them to eat later.

The ride across the plains had been as close to hell as Lost Woman had ever come. She was tied on the horse and the horse led on a rope. She was not allowed to get off for twelve hours. She had relieved herself on the horse's back as the Indians screamed and laughed.

Her dress had been torn off and she was naked to the waist. She was humiliated and prayed that they would kill her.

Lost Woman stared at the brilliant night sky again. She saw a falling star streak across the sky. Once she had wondered about them, about the stars in the night sky. Now she didn't bother. She was beyond wondering. Now she was thinking more and more about taking her own life.

A knife. There was always a knife available she could get. She could cut her wrists and go to sleep — and simply never wake up. Yes, the more she thought about it, the more she longed for release. A release from this living hell.

Perhaps tomorrow. She would steal a small

knife as she helped get the evening meal. Then that night. . . . For just a moment she wondered if it was right? Was it right for her to kill herself? The church had said something about that, but it had been so long ago. So tremendously long ago!

Lost Woman put her head down on the coarse hair of the old buffalo robe and cried. For a moment it surprised her. No Indian had seen her cry after the first week. She had not cried for a long time.

Lost Woman did not know if she were crying because she was in a hopeless situation, or if she cried because tomorrow night she might be able to kill herself.

CHAPTER SEVEN

Monday morning when Colt walked into the headquarters office, Major Longley was talking to the Officer of the Day. The adjutant motioned for Colt to come over.

"Bit of a problem here, Colonel. Figure you should have the say on it." He motioned to the Second Lieutenant who looked up at the Fort Commander.

"Sir, we've been having a group of people demonstrating outside the fort. There are four of them, two men and two women. They're walking back and forth across the road from the fort and carrying placards with slogans printed on them."

"Is one of the men named Dobson, the one who came to see me yesterday?" Colonel Harding asked.

Major Longley grinned and nodded. "Afraid so, sir. He's a persistent crackpot. What should we do about them, sir?"

Colt took a walk out to the guard house and watched the marchers fifty feet beyond the enlisted men's company kitchens and mess hall.

The signs were poorly lettered, but he could make out what two of them said. "Stop Killing Indians," and "Sand Creek Massacre."

Colt scratched his jaw and scuffed his boots in the dry soil. "Can't see how they're hurting anything. Every man in this country has the right to protest. As long as they stay off the fort area, leave them alone."

Colt paused. "Major, see if you can dig up four cinnamon rolls somewhere and take them and four cups of coffee out to the marchers. They must be ready for a good hot cup of coffee by now."

Whit Longley grinned. "The old kill them with kindness treatment, right, Colonel?"

"Can't hurt."

Back in the headquarters, the telegraph clerk came out of his small room with a message. He was a corporal, and had some of the toughest duty on the post. For eight hours a day he had to tend to the wire, and pick off every message aimed at Fort Larson, and those which he thought the commander and the officers would be interested in.

"Message for you, sir, from Omaha Department Headquarters."

Colt took the paper on which the clerk had

printed out the words as they came over the wire letter by letter into his office. He read it twice, then told Sergeant McIntyre to have Major Longley come in as soon as he got back from his mission of mercy.

Colt read the wire again.

TO: ALL FORTS ALONG THE UNION PACIFIC TRACKS FROM FORT MCPHERSON TO FORT FRED STEELE. UPSURGE OF INDIAN ACTIVITY DISRUPTING TRAIN SCHEDULES, DESTROYING TRACKS, EVEN HARASSING SOME TRAINS. FOR THE NEXT TWO WEEKS LAUNCH A TWENTY MILE PATROL DAILY ALONG TRACKS EACH WAY FROM YOUR FORT. WATCH FOR ANY INDIAN ACTIVITY AND REPULSE SAME. ANY INDIAN PRESENCE NEAR TRACKS CON-SIDERED TO BE A THREAT AND ENGAGE-MENT WITH THE PURSUIT OF HOSTILES AUTHORIZED.

ACTIVATE FIRST PATROLS UPON RECEIPT OF THIS NOTICE. REPORT ALL INDIAN ACTIVITY AT ONCE BY WIRE TO THIS HEADQUARTERS. FORTS STEELE, SANDERS, LARSON AND D.A. RUSSEL ALSO TO SEND PATROLS EVERY THREE DAYS TWENTY MILES DUE NORTH OF THESE INSTALLATIONS TO OBSERVE INDIAN ACTIVITY. REPORT ANYTHING OUT OF THE

ORDINARY SUCH AS LARGE GATHERINGS OR PREPARATIONS FOR WAR.

SIGNED: COLONEL J. RANDOLPH, ADJUTANT, DEPARTMENT OF THE PLATTE, OMAHA.

Whit Longley read the wire when he came back. He grunted and dropped in a chair.

"Looks like we got some planning to do. Daily patrols twenty miles each way. That's horse soldiers. If we split our six troops into two platoons each we can cut down the frequency to a little over one patrol unit per week."

"We'll have sixteen patrols a week for twelve units," Colt said. "Good, get it organized and send out the first patrols each way and north within two hours."

The Major left to get the troops into action. Colt stopped by his desk and Major Longley looked up scowling.

"We're short on officers in three of our troops. Means we'll have to switch some infantry officers with cavalry experience over to take the second half of the troops."

"No problem, we'll send them along the tracks."

Longley looked up. "I've set Strachey and half of C Troop for the twenty miles north patrol. Should I put him back on the tracks?"

Colt pondered it a minute. "Let him go, shouldn't be any trouble out there. Might give him some confidence."

The three patrols rode out less than an hour and a half after the telegram came into the fort headquarters. Colt made sure that Sergeant Troob was along with C Troop just in case he would be needed.

Major Whit Longley watched Colt staring after C Troop as it moved north toward town.

"One thing that's hard to get used to, isn't it? Watching the troops ride out, instead of leading them."

"Damn hard. Near impossible. I'll probably go on the next run north in three days."

First Sergeant Theodore Troob rode beside Lieutenant Strachey at the head of their compact columns of fours as they left the northern part of the small town of Larson City. It wasn't much of a town, but for this part of Wyoming Territory it was a metropolis.

He watched his Troop Commander from the corner of his eye. The two men had never exchanged a word about the previous patrol when they had chased the hostiles and almost ridden into a trap that could have slaughtered the whole troop.

That very fact made Troob even more convinced that Strachey should no longer have command of the troop. The man was not mentally stable enough to command men in a field combat situation.

They moved out smartly, angled away from the river to the right and away from the Union Pacific railroad tracks. The other patrol on the westbound leg of the track patrol was in sight for more than two hours as they both worked north on their assigned routes.

They were in the middle of the Larson River Valley, here more than 22 miles wide before it came up to the first low ridge of the Larson Mountains on the east. There was no need to put outriders in place. Here there was no danger. Still, Sergeant Troob kept his gaze sweeping the valley ahead and on both sides.

They rode for ten miles and then came close to the first ridge that led into the Larson Mountain foothills. Troob had been angling the column slightly to the left and around the ridge.

"We better stay to our due north course," Lieutenant Strachey said. "We'll go up and over that ridge at that low place just ahead."

"Yes, sir," Troob said, wondering why the officer was hanging on to the strict letter of the orders. North could be all sorts of places on a map, why charge up a ridge that you didn't have to?

Troob sent an outrider on the right side with instructions to report any sign of Indians at once. They rode another half mile and Troob turned to his Commander.

"Sir, I'm going to check out that area beyond the ridge before we charge into it. Might as well know what's over there so we can be ready."

The Lieutenant nodded and Troob spurred ahead. He galloped for a hundred yards, then angled up the hill at the low place on the ridge where they would pass through. His outrider was picking his way up the side of the steeper slope.

Troob came to the top of the rise and paused as he looked over.

"I'll be damned," he said. In the half mile wide valley that stretched between this ridge and the higher ones into the Larson Mountains to the east, grazed a herd of at least a thousand buffalo. He hadn't seen that many buffs for months, and none at all on this side of the Larson Mountains that swept down eastward into the great plains.

A herd like that could attract the Indian population for 50 miles around. Sergeant Troob lifted his field glasses and checked out the thin line of brush that must follow a small stream down through the long valley. He could see no tipis and breathed a sigh of relief.

At least no Indians had set up hunting camps down there getting ready to start a kill.

The one thing they didn't need to do was tangle with a hunting camp. The Cheyenne were overly protective when it came to their buffalo killing. He could understand it since their whole livelihood depended on the shaggy creatures.

Troob checked for as far up the stream as he could see but nowhere did he find the cones of the Indian shelters. Still, it would be better to leave the valley alone. Five miles farther up they could swing over the ridge.

Sergeant Troob got back to the main body about the time his outrider did. The trooper had seen the same herd of buffs. The sergeant rode up to C Troop Commander.

"Sir, just over the ridge is a small valley that is full of buffalo. I'd figure more than a thousand buffs over there. There's a good chance there's a band or two or maybe three of Cheyenne or Arapaho camped nearby getting ready for an early buffalo hunt. It would be better for us to go north another five miles before we ride over the ridge."

Lieutenant Strachey stared at him. "Sergeant, what did our orders say for this patrol?"

"To go north, sir."

"As I remember the wording it was *due north*. That doesn't mean circling around a

spot where there just might be some hostiles. We'll go over the ridge as planned, Sergeant."

The ex-colonel sat on his horse without
moving. He watched the officer who stared
back hard.

"You have some trouble with that order,
Sergeant?"

"It is not what I recommend, sir."

"That's right, Sergeant. Your suggestion is
not taken, I'm giving the orders here. We'll go
over the ridge at this point and complete our
mission as ordered."

"Yes, sir." Troob turned and waved the
men ahead, pointing them over the low pass
toward the valley.

Ten minutes later they topped the ridge
and looked down. Some of the troopers had
never seen a herd of buffalo before. The
troopers had come on the herd about at the
middle. The grazing animals were strung out
over a mile of the lush valley. Sergeant Troob
turned the column so it would angle down the
side of the low ridge and not ride into the
middle of the herd.

"Sergeant, we need to be in the valley to be
moving north."

"Yes sir, but have you ever ridden into a
herd of buffalo like that before? We could lose
every horse and man we have. Buffs just hate

horses for some reason. If we got them critters into a stampede we could all go down under their sharp hooves and come up mincemeat."

As First Lieutenant Rodney Strachey looked at the milling, munching mass of buffalo two hundred yards below them, his lower lip began to tremble. He firmed his jaw and nodded at his Sergeant.

"Yes, noted. Continue on this path."

They angled for another 10 minutes, and 20 minutes later they had made it past the slowly grazing animals and swung down into the valley. The small brush shrouded stream swung wide at this point and the men of C Troop approached it, electing to splash across rather than detour a quarter of a mile around the twisting, slowly running creek.

There was no warning.

From behind them 50 Cheyenne warriors burst out of the screen of brush and charged the troopers. The cavalrymen were less than 50 yards away when the first rifle shot sounded from the hostiles.

Sergeant Troob looked first at Lieutenant Strachey. His chin quiver had claimed his whole face now and he slumped over the saddle and charged up the valley toward the creek and its cover of brush and away from the hostiles.

Sergeant Troob assumed command at once.

"Spread out, remain mounted and fire at will!" Sergeant Troob bellowed.

A dozen shots sounded, then more came as the troopers uncovered each other to get clear shots at the onrushing hostiles.

The 20 rifles blasting lead into the charging mass of Indians and their war ponies, took effect quickly. The charge broke off 30 yards away and swung downstream.

"Into the brush!" Troob barked as the rifles stopped firing. Troob looked for wounded. He saw two men holding arms and another one had fallen over his saddle and clung to the neck of his horse. A buddy held the man on his horse.

"Move it!" Troob bellowed. "Into the brush before they come back. They will be back." The men swung their mounts and galloped for the brush. Once inside the slight cover, Sergeant Troob calmed the men.

"Dismount and form a line of skirmishers along the edge of the brush line. Fifth man take horses to the far side of the brush and stay with them. I want a casualty report. How is that badly wounded man?"

"I'll make it, Sarge," a voice called. "Got me in the side, but I'll live."

There were two more men hit by rifle fire,

both in the arm, but all three were on the firing line.

"The hostiles will be back. This is probably a hunting party just not quite ready for the hunt. But neither are they ready for war. They'll attack again. This time I want you to concentrate on knocking down their ponies. Shoot for the horses' heads. A Cheyenne without his horse is only half a warrior."

He turned and saw Corporal Connell. He lowered his voice to a whisper. "Connell, get mounted and find Lieutenant Strachey. He should be upstream in the brush or near it. Find him and bring him back here. He went crazy." The Corporal ran for his horse.

Sergeant Troob hurried to the front of the brush, found a spot behind a fallen cottonwood tree and made sure his Spencer Carbine repeater was primed and full of rounds. He had one in the chamber and seven in the tube. Over his back he carried a Blakeslee Quickloader with 13 tubes each loaded with seven rounds for the Spencer.

In front of the troopers about 200 yards, the Cheyenne came out of the brush in a "V" front they often used and charged at the men of C Troop. Most of the 18 men had found good cover to protect themselves. They would be exposed only when they lifted up to fire, or fired around a tree or log.

"Hold fire until my command!" Sergeant Troob thundered so all his men could hear him.

The "V" of more than 40 Cheyenne charged forward. When they were 50 yards away, Troob gave the command to fire. All 18 carbines blasted within a second or two. The leading man in the "V" was blown off his mount with three slugs in his chest. The next two Indians went down as their horses screamed and died. Two more horses stumbled and fell and the charge was broken as the Cheyenne again turned and rode upstream.

Corporal Connell came up leading Lieutenant Strachey's horse. He tied up the mounts at the back of the brush and slid down beside Sergeant Troob.

"Found him, Sarge, but he wouldn't move. He was curled into a ball behind a rock upstream about a hundred yards. He kept whispering something about 'Nanny won't find me here,' whatever the hell that means.

"Sarge, the front of his pants were all wet and I smelled something foul. I'm certain he shit his pants."

"Not a word to anyone, Corporal. Get your carbine on line. We'll get the lieutenant when this little fracas is over."

The Cheyenne made one more try, but this time they stopped a hundred yards away and fired the five or six rifles they had. When they took return fire and lost another man and three more horses went down they pulled back.

"They're done," Sergeant Troob said. He pointed to a tall, slender southerner beside him. "Jackson, you hold the fort here until I get back. Shouldn't be any problem." He motioned to Corporal Connell and they took off at a trot upstream toward the C Troop Commander.

He still huddled behind the big rock. As the two men ran up he glanced at them in terror, then saw their uniforms and seemed to recover. He nodded at them, stood and slapped his campaign hat free of some twigs and leaves.

"Well, now, Sergeant. You see I have the situation well in hand. We've checked out this area, I'd say it's time we swing back into the main valley and continue on our nearly northern course."

"Yes, sir. The troops are waiting slightly downstream. We took your horse there for safekeeping."

"Naturally. We can't afford to lose any horses on a simple little patrol like this." He turned and walked ahead of them downstream. He made no mention of his urine stained blue trousers or the fecal odor that came from them.

Corporal Connell looked at Troob and lifted his brows.

"Talk about it later," Troob said. "Now let's get out of these hunting grounds while the getting is possible."

Back at the line of skirmishers, Jackson reported all was quiet. The man hit in the side had been patched up as good as was possible. The bleeding had been stopped with a folded kerchief, and two more and an undershirt had been torn up to make bandages. The men hit in the arms had their wounds bandaged securely and were ready to move.

Lieutenant Strachey caught his horse and moved upstream in the brush. When he came back he smelled slightly less powerful, but the odor couldn't be entirely removed.

"Sergeant, form up the men and let's move out straight up the ridge and down the other side."

"Yes sir," Troob said and had the men underway two minutes later.

They went over the ridge without opposition, and down the far side, then turned north close along the ridgeline. The other patrol was not more than three or four miles away working north along the south side of the U.P. tracks.

It was nearly two that afternoon when Lieutenant Strachey called a halt.

"Tell the men they can eat their rations and build fires if they wish. We'll be here for an hour to let the horses rest. We're at the twenty mile point. This afternoon we'll return to the fort."

"Yes sir," Sergeant Troob said.

As the men ate their hardtack and salt pork that had been issued, and boiled coffee in their big metal cups, they talked about their Commanding Officer. Those men who didn't see him turn and run from the fight soon learned of it from the other troopers. By the time the noon rest was over, every man in the platoon knew about the Lieutenant's wet and dirty pants.

All the way back to the fort that afternoon, Sergeant Troob argued and fought with himself about just how to present the situation to Colonel Harding. He had to know. The Lieutenant should not command men in the field ever again. But how could he make the Fort Commander understand that so he would act?

CHAPTER EIGHT

It was fully dark when C Troop entered the parade grounds. Sergeant Troob brought them into a four horse column front and Lieutenant Strachey dismissed them. He had made no comment or move concerning the three wounded men.

Sergeant Troob called the names of the three wounded and they rode to the end of the quartermaster building where a small medical unit had been built. He took the men inside, then led the horses to the stables where he assigned two men to unsaddle the three mounts and rub them down.

When Troob was sure his three men were being cared for, he went directly to the fort headquarters. Major Longley was still there. He took one look at the anger on the Sergeant's face.

"It happened again, Sergeant Troob?"

"Yes. At least no one was killed. He rode off and hid when we were attacked."

"Good God, not again." Whit Longley

stood nursing some old rheumatism. "Sit down, Troob. I'll go get the Colonel. This will spoil his evening, but we all know how important it is."

A few minutes later, Colt had heard what happened on the patrol.

"So it wasn't a case of bad judgment, poor soldiering," Colt said. "It was simply stark, uncontrollable terror."

"Yes, sir. I'm not sure he even knows what happened. When we brought him back he acted as if nothing had taken place. He had no idea there was a fight with the Cheyenne or that any of the men were wounded. By now every man in the troop knows what the Lieutenant did out there."

"Thanks, Troob, for taking over and getting those men out of there. This is on your shoulders, you know. We have only you to thank for saving that platoon."

"If it hadn't been me, somebody else would have got them out safely."

"Not without a lot of dead and wounded. I put in my authorization today to promote you to Second Lieutenant on a 'field necessity and in close action with the enemy.' "

"Thanks for trying. Can't possibly go through."

"We'll see. In the meantime, I'm relieving Strachey. I can't let him take the field again."

"You could have a revolt on your hands sir, if he tried to take C Troop out again."

"Troob, would you go with him if I did?" Colt asked.

"Yes, but I have your standing order to fall back on. The men don't know that. There would be problems. Best idea is to move him to administration or something, as you're doing." Troob shook his head. "Sir, Excuse me. I didn't mean to be presumptive. Old habits die hard, sir."

Colt laughed. "Troob, since I've seen your record, I consider you to be equal in rank with me. So no apologies are needed, or wanted. I wish I could give C Troop to you, but that wouldn't work either. You know the officer/enlisted problem."

"Yes, sir. If that commission did, by some act of God, come through, I'd have to be transferred, correct?"

"Yes, to a new post."

Troob shrugged. "That's the army. I should be used to it by now. Can we expect a new C Troop Commander, sir?"

Colt looked at his adjutant. "We'll be working out something tonight and you should know by noon."

"May I tell the troops?"

Colt stood and walked around his desk. He stared at the two lamps that lit the office and at last nodded.

"Yes, Troob, call them together tonight and tell them plain and simple that the Lieutenant suffered — battle fatigue, let's call it, and that he's being replaced in the morning with a new Commander. That should cut down on the rumors and gossip."

Sergeant McIntyre came in and said he had sent for Lieutenant Strachey. Sergeant Troob saluted and Colt returned the honors and the trooper left the office.

"That was the easy part," Colt said. "What can we tell Strachey?" When Major Longley shook his head, Colt sat back down. "I was asking myself, I guess. The only thing is to do what I would want done for me. The truth, straight from the shoulder, offer him the chance to resign with no unfavorable report on either of these last two incidents. He should accept that."

Just then they heard the outer door open and then close. Voices sounded in the other office, then Lieutenant Strachey came in. His uniform was not spotless as it usually was. He had changed clothes since the patrol, but looked tired. For the first time Colt could remember, the man did not have his hair combed perfectly. There was a smudge of dirt on his right cheek.

"You wanted to see me, sir?" C Troop's

Commander asked.

"Yes, Strachey. Sit down. Major, I'll talk to you later. See what you can do on that roster."

Longley nodded and left the room, almost closing the door.

"Lieutenant Strachey, we have a serious problem here and the only way I know how to solve it is to be honest, be sure we both understand the facts, and then try to work out a solution."

"Is it something I did, sir?"

"Are you aware of any problems in your command of C Troop?"

"None, sir."

"Did you go on patrol today with half of C Troop, Lieutenant?"

"Yes, sir."

"Please give me a thumbnail sketch of what happened."

"It will be in the report in the morning. But . . . well, we left the fort before noon, headed north along the ridge of the Larson Mountains, followed it up to what I figured was twenty miles, then had a food break, rested the horses for an hour and returned to post."

"That was it?"

"Yes, sir."

"Did you see any hostiles?"

"No, sir."

"Did you see any buffalo?"

"Buffalo? No, not a one."

"Did you have a skirmish with any Cheyenne warriors?"

"No, sir."

Colt called for coffee. Sergeant McIntyre almost always had a pot boiling or heating on a small stove in the outer office, winter or summer. He brought in a pot and two cups. Colt poured a cup for the other man, then himself.

"Lieutenant Strachey, why did you go to West Point, and join the army?"

"I wanted to, I worked hard for an appointment. Besides, it's a long tradition in my father's family."

"Your father was in the army?"

"Yes, sir. He was a Major General, but died in an accident three years before the Civil War began."

"If you weren't in the army, what kind of work would you want to do?"

"I've always wanted to be an artist. I draw and do paintings now and then when I have time."

Colt stood and walked around the desk and stared down at the man. "Lieutenant Strachey, were you lying to me about what happened on the patrol today?"

"Lying? No sir! It was an uneventful ride

out and back. You can ask any of my men."

"You honestly believe that?"

"Absolutely. I'll stake my reputation as an officer on that fact, Colonel."

"That's what I was afraid of," Colt said, easing back. He went behind his desk and sat in his chair. "First Lieutenant Rodney Strachey, you are hereby relieved of your command of C Troop and are confined to quarters until further notice. If you wish, you may ask for a court martial or you may resign from the army quietly, with no charges brought, and no adverse records showing in your personnel file."

Strachey jolted backward as if he had been struck.

"What. . . . what. . . ." He shook his head. "Resign? I don't understand. What have I done that's so awful? How can I be charged with such a serious crime? What do you say I've done?"

"Will you believe me if I tell you?"

"Yes, if you prove what you say I did."

"You suffered some kind of a mental breakdown, evidently. This afternoon you led your troops into a valley where a thousand buffalo were grazing and right into at least one Cheyenne hunting party. The warriors attacked your patrol without warning. As soon as the attack started, you bolted and rode away and hid until the skirmish was over.

"At some point you lost control of your bladder and you also shit your pants. Sergeant Troob and Corporal Connell found you shaking and doubled into a ball behind a large rock. After the battle was over you acted as if it hadn't taken place. Three of your men were wounded in the exchange. Sergeant Troob took over command of the troop, fought off the hostiles, rescued you and led the men out of the valley and back on the mission."

"Liars! Any man who said that happened is a damned liar." Strachey came half out of his chair, his face angry, suddenly red and his eyes wild.

"Then there are twenty-three men in C Troop who are liars. They all saw you bolt and run. They fought off the hostiles without your assistance. And right now three of your men are in the medical offices with bullet wounds. How can you explain the bullet wounds if there was no battle with the hostiles?"

"They are all liars. The wounds are faked. You can't tell if an arm or a leg is shot when it's all bandaged up. I had a sniveling mama's boy private try to get out of duty that way once. . . ."

"Lieutenant Strachey, do you remember

99

several days ago when I went along with your troop when we investigated the track burning and disruption? We chased the hostiles?"

"Yes, of course I remember."

"That day you almost led your company into a trap. That day when the hostiles attacked us you froze and pretended the enemy wasn't there. I saw all of that with my own eyes, Strachey. Are you going to call me a liar as well?"

"There was no contact with the hostiles today. Those men are lying. I don't know why, but they are liars!"

Colt went back in front of Strachey.

"On your feet, soldier!" Colt snapped. Strachey came to attention in front of his Colonel.

"Lieutenant Strachey, you are relieved of your command of C Troop, and confined to quarters except for regular mess. We'll talk about this tomorrow after you've had time to think it over."

Colt went to the door and signalled to Sergeant McIntyre. "Sergeant, would you escort Lieutenant Strachey over to his quarters."

Strachey looked at Colt with an expression the Fort Commander couldn't read. It was not anger or hatred, but it was not a pleasant emotion either. He watched Colt for a few seconds, then turned, put on his hat and walked out the door with Sergeant McIntyre following him.

Whit Longley shook his head. "I heard most of it through the door. The man would not admit that some of his men were wounded today?"

"He evidently blocks it all out, withdraws from anything that is going to be so painful that it would stagger him. By hiding from it, it can't hurt him. When the danger is gone, he snaps back, has no memory of the lost minutes, hours, even days I would imagine, and functions as if it didn't happen. To his way of thinking, it *didn't* happen."

"You saying the man is crazy?"

"Close enough. All we can do is send a sealed dispatch to Major Randolph at Department Headquarters asking what to do with him. I'd think they'll want to examine him in Omaha and maybe Chicago."

"I'll get a letter ready for your signature in the morning. I've found a man for C Troop. He's had experience with a cavalry unit at Fort Leavenworth. Right now he's second in command of Easy Troop. I'll move him up to C Troop as soon as I can have Sergeant McIntyre go find him. This puts us another officer short."

"That's what happens when an army goes from two-point-one million men down to twenty-five thousand. Lots of Generals and Colonels and Majors, but damn few Second Lieutenants. We always need more Second Lieutenants."

"About Strachey, is he dangerous? Do you think he'll hurt anyone, even himself?"

"Not a chance. Why should he do that? He can't remember doing anything wrong, and he knows that he's as sane as you or I. No, he'll be fine. We just have to keep him in his quarters until Division tells us what to do. Three or four days I'd think should do it."

"Sorry to ruin your evening this way. At least nobody got killed this afternoon."

"Thanks to Colonel Troob," Colt said and waved. Maybe he could salvage something of the evening yet. He had planned playing a tough game of gin rummy with Doris.

At least it would take his mind off Strachey. What a shame. He remembered Strachey talking about the Civil War and how he had been bloodied there in some of the late fighting just before the surrender. That probably was a fabrication as well.

At least he was stopped before he created a disaster and cost the lives of 30 or 40 men.

CHAPTER NINE

The next morning about ten A.M. when the first patrol went out to work the southern 20 mile run along the tracks, they found a protester shouting at them, carrying his sign about killing Indians.

"Woman killers!" J. Thorndike Dobson screamed at the men of B Troop as they walked their horses past him. "Murderers! Killers of a whole race of people."

Some of the troops shouted back at him, but that made J. Thorndike even angrier. The young lieutenant at the head of the column looked away and stopped the troop. A moment later two men leaped off their horses, raced to the civilian and stripped off his clothing leaving him naked. They took his clothes, jeered at him and mounted up. Almost at once the half a troop moved off to the south.

J. Thorndike screamed at them, then ran toward his house furiously trying to cover himself. At last he found some branches with

103

heavy leaves from a small tree and hurried away.

"The President is going to hear about this!" J. Thorndike bellowed after the patrol. Two men in the rear ranks raised his shirt and pants and waved them at him. They didn't drop the clothing until they were two miles down the tracks to the east.

It was over an hour later that Colt heard about the spectacle near the fort. Major Longley had a complete report on it because he knew that J. Thorndike would be back. The adjutant showed the report to Colt as soon as he came to his office.

"I put a draft of a possible letter about Lieutenant Strachey on your desk. Then here's something else. We had an 'incident' this morning, with your good friend J. Thorndike Dobson."

Colt read the paper and snorted. "Damn! That young Lieutenant Newton is going to have some explaining to do." Colt grinned. "But it served that Dobson right. He got a little irritation back for a change."

"At least you'll know all the facts when he comes storming in here — as soon as he finds some pants."

Both men laughed.

"Hear anything from Strachey?"

Whit Longley nodded. "I've had two notes

104

delivered by enlisted men from Strachey so far. He wants to talk to you again to make certain you understand his position."

"His position isn't important. His *condition* is the serious part and I don't know what else to do. Tell him I'll see him here at one o'clock."

A half hour later J. Thorndike Dobson came steaming into the Fort Commander's office. He looked at Major Longley and held up his hand when Sergeant McIntyre started to speak. Dobson marched to Colt's door and pushed it open. His fists were set on his hips as he stalked into the big office.

"This time you've gone too far!" Dobson shrilled. "I'm charging those two soldiers with assault and battery and I'm suing them for a hundred thousand dollars. Do you know what they did to me right out there on public land, well off the boundary of the fort?"

"Sit down, Mr. Dobson. Sit down. Can I get you a cup of coffee?"

"Goddamnit, no! I want some justice, not coffee. Do you know what your men did? I want that Lieutenant stripped of his rank and put in prison as well. He permitted the assault to take place, so ultimately it's his fault. I'm suing him as well. And my lawyer says I can sue all three with strong and actionable legal standing."

"Mr. Dobson, it was just a prank. Were you injured?"

"Well, no."

"Did a lot of people see you naked? I understand you covered yourself with branches and leaves."

"Of course I covered myself."

"Then I don't see where you have much of a legal case. You provoked the men, two of them removed your clothing. I think you'd be laughed out of court."

"Not so. My lawyer is the best. We'll get our hundred thousand dollars, because he says the army is liable for the actions of its men against civilians. I want a copy of any reports written on the incident. You have one already I would guess. I want it, now."

"Impossible," Major Longley said from the open doorway. "That report is army property and can't be released without authorization from the Army's Commanding General."

"We'll get it. I'm going to name both of you men as co-conspirators in the attack since your men are your responsibility. I'm writing the President, and two U.S. Senators I know. You'll be hearing from my lawyer!"

J. Thorndike jammed on his hat and walked out of the office.

Colt looked at his adjutant. "Do you think he'll do it, sue us?"

"Yes, I'm certain he will. He's been mortified and he probably has a good case. My first thought was to transfer the two enlisted men involved to Maine or Florida, but that might look like an admission of guilt."

"Have you heard of civilians suing army personnel before?" Colt asked.

"Oh, yes, when they are in town, on their own. But I don't recall any time enlisted men were sued when they were under army command. I'll make some inquiries, and contact Omaha."

"No, not anyone outside of camp. I want to squash this right here if we can."

"Yes, that's the better idea."

Major Longley left and Colt dug into the paperwork that was required of him as the Commandant.

That afternoon, promptly at one P.M., Lieutenant Strachey walked quietly into the office and asked if he could see Colonel Harding.

Sergeant McIntyre took him to the open door and when Colt looked up, he nodded.

"Yes, Strachey, come in. Sergeant, please close the door. I don't want to be disturbed for anything short of war."

Colt poured the officer a cup of coffee, army black, and settled back in his chair.

"Lieutenant, have you thought over what

107

we talked about yesterday?"

"Yes, sir. I have scrubbed my memory, gone over everything in the most minute detail. I can recall nothing that you say happened yesterday. Now that I consider all you told me, I can only reason that I may have had some kind of a temporary lapse. It would be like the lights going off and everything going black in a formerly lighted room."

"Then you're saying that what I related to you could have happened?"

"No, sir. I'm not ready to admit that yet. What I propose is a test. I want to go out on the next patrol sent to chase the hostiles. Not in a command position, as an observer. I could even serve as a trooper. I need to test myself. Is that too much to ask?"

Colt considered it. "That way you would put no one in any danger, would not have command. But what would you do then? How would you react if you found out that it was true, that you simply could not face the enemy in battle?"

"I don't know, Colonel. I've never really been in fighting situations before I came here. I lied to you about the Civil War. I was trying to be the perfect officer, and officers must function well in engagements with the enemy. I apologize."

"If you find that you panic again, that the

terror is too much for your mind to accept, then will you resign?"

"Absolutely. If I'm a liability instead of an asset in a fighting situation, I should not have command of troops in the field. And, since the army rewards only its fighting officers with promotions, I would have no future in the army. My mother expects me to be a general in seven more years. I'll never make it."

"What about your painting?"

"Yes, that would be my next consideration. I . . . I don't exactly need to work for a living. I have trust funds and investments. I wouldn't have to sell my paintings, is what I'm trying to say."

Colt lit his pipe. He had taken up the habit recently and enjoyed it now and then. He pulled hard on it to get the tamped in tobacco lighted, then held the heavy briar by the bowl.

"Strachey, I'll be honest with you. I don't think you should go out and test yourself. It could be dangerous. I haven't made up my mind yet, but I'm leaning against the idea. I'll let you know for sure in two or three days. Now, this is a good chance for you to do some painting. Do you have enough light in your quarters?"

"Yes, enough light. Colonel, I need this test for my own peace of mind. Please let me make it."

Colt stood and nodded. "I'll consider it, Lieutenant. That will be all."

The officer stood, started to salute, then stopped and walked out the door.

Colt sat there puffing his pipe when Major Longley walked in.

"That letter about the field commission for Troob got off in the dispatch case on the noon train east. How did it go with the Lieutenant?"

"Strachey wants one more chance to prove himself. He offered to go into action against the hostiles as a trooper."

"No command authority?"

"None. I told him I'd let him know. He wants to deliberately test himself."

Major Longley rubbed his jaw. "Damned if I wouldn't want to do the same thing if I blacked out that way. Damned if I wouldn't."

Forty-five miles above Larson City on Tall Grass Creek that flowed into the Larson River, Brave Bull sat inside his tipi staring at the flames of a small fire.

The young warriors were angry. He was angry. The Pony Soldiers had clearly beat them in the battle by the valley of the buffalo. He had taken the men on a searching mission to find an Arapaho hunting camp. They would destroy it! But the Pony Soldiers showed up first and frightened away the Arapaho band.

His band had suffered four dead in the confrontation. The shoots-many-times-rifles were deadly. No spear or bow and arrow could win. He must get more rifles for his men.

He must also come up with a raid that would stamp out the memory of the last defeat. Something to fire their imaginations, to win their loyalty.

It was summer camp, it was time for war. He would give the young men war. They would make a raid on the Pony Soldiers' wooden tipis! They would ride like the wind in the night and come on the fort in the small hours of morning, set it on fire, steal their horses and some of their women, and rush back to the safety of the high Larson River!

Yes! It could be done! Now was the time of the dark moon. That would help. He had sensed the coming of a storm. It would be there in two days. Much lightning and thunder and furious rain. Cheyenne rode best in the rain!

Brave Bull called in the medicine man. He would need his best magic for this attack. It was by far the most ambitious of any of his raids in the past. He would take every warrior who could ride, and many of the young teenage boys not yet full warriors. He needed as great a number as possible.

Every rifle and revolver they had captured and bought must be working and must fire and kill the hated Pony Soldiers. He reveled in his new purpose, his face alive, his dark eyes watching the fire and seeing the whole of the battle.

Yes, it would be good.

The medicine man put the entire band through a ritual that would almost guarantee a successful raid. Then Brave Bull stripped to his breechclout and walked high on the ridge line and prostrated himself on a slanting rock and let Brother Wind and Sister Chill do what it could to him all night. He didn't sleep or nap and rose with Father Sun, energized and ready to lead the attack.

He announced that they would ride about noon the next day to avenge the four warriors who fell at the buffalo valley.

"We will burn the wooden tipis to the ground! We will slaughter the rabbits they call Pony Soldiers. We will take their women and young girls as slaves and ride home on the wind and defeat any attempt to follow us!"

The warriors' voices rose in a surging chant of "Yes, yes, yes!"

Two Dogs screamed with the other warriors, then hurried to his tipi to prepare for the fight. First he would do his special ritual that had brought him bravery and good magic in

112

all of his battles during the past year.

He caught his slave by her hand and pushed her toward the tipi. First Flower watched him and growled, but he spat angry words at his first wife, then went into the tipi and stripped the dress off Lost Woman, pushed her down on his bed and took her hard and fast the way he would a white woman he had just captured.

She did not resist. For a moment he saw anger in her eyes, but then it faded and he pumped harder until his loins exploded and he knew that he would have a successful raid. They would leave about midday and ride through good cover, slipping up on the fort, then resting their horses until the attack came deep into Friend Night.

Two Dogs smiled. Perhaps he could capture another slave woman!

CHAPTER TEN

Fifty-two Cheyenne warriors and youths of 15 who were almost warriors, rode through the Wyoming afternoon moving south. They kept their route through the foothills as much as possible, utilizing cover and concealment whenever they could as they worked closer and closer to the white man's wooden tipi fort.

They carried a dozen fire boxes, small containers of sand that held burning coals from their ceremonial fire. These coals would be used to fan into flame and burn down the Pony Soldiers' wooden tipis. It would be a glorious raid!

Brave Bull swung them away east another ridge as they came closer to the big White Eye camp on the Larson River. Few of the warriors had seen so many of the wooden tipis in one place. They stretched for half a mile and extended for a quarter of that distance on each side. It was dark by the time they came that far, but they could see many, many lights.

They passed them by since they didn't come for the civilian White Eyes.

The wind, which had been blowing in from the west, came harder now. Far off they could see the gods throwing great sheets of fire at each other. Now and then one would throw a crooked lance that would strike the ground.

The wind increased and Brave Bull smiled, knowing the storm was coming quickly now.

Brave Bull looked at the village and decided there were more than 200 of the wooden shelters. How could so many White Eyes live so close together? They must stay there all the time. How could they keep enough graze for their horses?

The raiders left the hills and moved closer to the town now, worked around the east side which was closest to the mountains, and at last just south of the village. Brave Bull saw the Pony Soldiers' wooden tipis. He had seen such places before when he went to the big peace conference.

The White chiefs had given them presents and then wanted them to make a mark on a piece of paper. Brave Bull did not know what the White Chiefs were saying, but he had to make his X to get the gifts, so he made the scratch. Everyone seemed pleased when he signed.

On the way back to his band from the conference, he and three of his braves had captured eight horses and one woman slave at a small ranch. It had been a good peace conference.

Now as they watched the fort, he held his young men in check. They had wanted to attack at once, but he made them wait. They moved around south of the fort and to the far side where Brave Bull himself crawled up until he could see the horses behind a flimsy wire fence.

He had brought two of the white man's axes. They would be used on the fence.

The first drops of rain came, gently at first, then whipped by the wind, it slashed at them. Cheyenne are not afraid of their Cousin Rain. It brought fresh grass for the war ponies. The rain came down more now and they sat beside their horses and waited. The worse the storm, the easier their job of stealing horses, taking women prisoners and burning down the buildings!

Six of the older warriors who were not interested in capturing horses would set the fires. They would blow their coals into flame against the paper weed and then light the corners of the one long building and the two smaller ones on the south side of the big square. It would be good.

They could hear the camp settling down.

The wind let up but the rain came stronger. Soon the Cheyenne were wet through, but they welcomed their Cousin Rain, and waited for the time to attack.

By midnight the rain eased a little, but the wind picked up and lightning flashed in the sky, one bolt struck one of the buildings but did not set it on fire.

Brave Bull gave the signal to the horsemen. They ran ahead, invisible in the blowing rain. They put the blade of the axe against the fence wire and another warrior pounded down on it with the blunt back of the axe head. The blow pinched the wire in half and the axe was raised to the next strand.

In three minutes they had the strands all cut and pulled back and wrapped around the other post leaving a gap of 20 feet in the fencing. The ten Cheyenne warriors moved silently in among the horses and gently urged them toward the gap. The mounts walked to it, then finding it open they moved out.

Just outside, a dozen Cheyenne warriors on their own war ponies herded the horses into a line and drove them north.

At the same time the horsemen began their work, Brave Bull ran with three other men to the corner of the long building and pulled dry paper weed from their buffalo robes and, using their bodies as shields, blew the coals into flame and started the paper weed on fire. The flames were pushed under the dry corner of the barracks where the officers had their quarters.

They protected the flames as they began to eat into the dry wood of the barracks where it was out of the rain and wind. When the fire took hold, they ran to the next building, the smaller one next to where the horses were fenced.

Three more men had attacked the other end of the long building with fire. Not a sound had been made so far. Some of the horses nickered and whinnied, but nothing unusual.

The interior guard who marched next to the paddock fence between the tack room and the enlisted men's barracks noticed the horses moving. He paid no attention to it at first, then on his second pass a minute later, he could see the horses all crowding toward the far fence. Through the rain and the wind pushed mists he saw the opening in the fence. A bolt of lightning flashed down and the guard saw horses running through the hole in the fence.

"Corporal of the Guard, post number six," the trooper bellowed.

The call was picked up by each post until it reached the guard house where the Sergeant of the Guard swore as he pulled on his poncho and ran out to post six.

At once he saw the trouble, and fired his pistol in the air three times. That brought out a dozen men from the guard house waiting for the next guard rotation. All carried carbines or rifles.

The Sergeant ran down past the stables and around to the fence. He was the first man killed when a Cheyenne rode up out of the rain and shot him through the heart with a broad tipped hunting arrow.

But the alarm was sounded. Men with weapons poured out of barracks. Some half dressed men, none with wet gear, rushed to the fence and closed the gap, pinning in two thirds of the horses: 150 horses were still inside. Rifles and carbines snapped rounds at the Cheyenne who charged away in the slashing rain, driving the stolen army mounts ahead of them.

Colt ran on the scene moments after the Sergeant had been killed. Three more enlisted were down from gunshot wounds. The fires were quickly found and put out with little or no damage.

Colt swore as he saw the way the hostiles had attacked them. He ordered A Troop to dress for foul weather and fall out in 30 minutes with full field gear and ready to ride. Colt would ride with them.

Captain Harold Garner commanded Able Troop. He was the only man at Captain's rank who ran a troop or infantry company at the fort. Colt figured he could have his men out quicker than anyone else. He found Major Longley.

"Get me the three best Indian scouts we have," he shouted through the wind and rain. "We have to get back those horses. Tell Captain Garner to take the first horses his men can saddle. We can't be particular which mounts we ride now. We have to move fast!"

It took them 40 minutes to get underway. The scouts brought along two lanterns each and wads of sulphur matches to light them.

Colt threw on clothes, found a poncho and rushed out to a horse that Sergeant McIntyre had saddled for him. He got ready before A Troop was fully assembled. It was a time of confusion. Squads usually riding together were not formed up at once, and stragglers hurried up to the tail end of the formation even as the call came for forward march.

As the formation moved out, another straggler came from near the stables area and rode smoothly into line. He had no rank showing, and wore a poncho as the rest of A Troop did. He settled into the formation without a word to the other men. Under the campaign hat pulled well down to shield his face, Lieutenant Strachey smiled grimly.

He would have his day in the field. He would find out for himself if he was a coward and had run away in the face of the enemy. If he did that, this time he would know, and this time he would quietly resign from the service, find a garret somewhere and begin to paint in earnest.

If his mother complained he would tell her to go to hell, and paint away. After all, no painter worth his brushes ever created anything without a lot of suffering. This would be part of his suffering before it was over, he was sure.

A Troop moved out of the fort past the paddock and to the north. The scouts had been out for 20 minutes, marking the trail.

One came back and talked to Captain Garner. He turned to Colt at his side.

"Limping Crow says they are driving the horses due north. They didn't even bother to go around town, went right down Wyoming Street. Limping Crow says they are driving the horses hard but will have to slow down soon. He figures they are about an hour ahead of us."

"They're pushing a herd of horses," Colt said. "We aren't. We should be able to outrun them. Pick up the pace, Captain, to six miles to the hour."

"I agree. Limping Crow, make damn sure you keep their trail. In this rain it won't last long."

Colt and A Troop slogged through the middle of Larson City and out the other side. Four of the army mounts were seen in the area, but they could be corralled later.

They pushed ahead. The rain slackened somewhat and a scout came back. The trail had slanted to the right toward the first range of hills of the Larson Mountains. Tracking was proving to be slower than they had figured with the hard rain. The hostiles were gaining slowly on them, moving further ahead.

Colt made sure his Spencer Carbine was loaded with eight rounds, and went back up front with the scout. They galloped for a quarter of a mile, then slowed and stopped. They both got off their horses and in the light of the lantern, Colt could make out plainly the multiple hoofprints in a soft spot on the valley floor.

They caught up with the connecting link scout who pointed where the trail had turned toward the ridge. The Indians chattered a minute and the one with a little English turned to Colt.

"He says they are slowing down, their ponies are getting tired. He figures they have about eighty army horses. But still they go faster than we do."

The rain had almost stopped now. Colt was trying to figure some way to overtake the hostiles. Without a lightning troop there was no better way than slogging it out. They had to be able to travel faster than a bunch of Cheyenne driving 80 horses. The problem was knowing for sure where their trail was.

He waited there for the rest of the patrol to catch up with him. Then he led them along the new trail that swept toward a low ridge.

"The scouts say there is no trap over the ridge. The Cheyenne have continued straight up the valley just beyond."

The troops welcomed the end of the rain. Colt checked his pocket watch with the flare of a match. It was just past two-thirty. They had been on the trail for an hour and a half.

Men began to take off their ponchos. If it wasn't raining outside, their sweat would gather inside the poncho and they would be wet again.

One man near the back kept on his poncho. Someone asked him about it and he shrugged but said nothing. He stared straight ahead and the others left him alone. The company was all mixed up and no one riding near the man knew who he was. Nor did they care.

They were wet, miserable and surely headed for a fight.

Here and there they found stray army mounts. Those that could be caught were trailed behind troopers on a lead line.

By three-thirty A.M. they had ten horses recaptured.

They pressed on.

It was just after four that morning when Limping Crow came up to the troop. They had kept to the one small valley since they went beyond the first ridge to the east. Now the Cheyenne drove the captured horses back over the ridge into the ever wider Larson River valley.

"Cheyenne stop three mile ahead," Limping Crow said. "Get ready to fight."

Captain Garner looked at Colt. "Don't sound like the Cheyennes that I know."

"Damned strange," Colt said. "What do you make of it, Limping Crow?"

"Trick. Cheyenne tricky."

The scout should know. Captain Garner said he was an Arapaho and hated the Cheyenne.

"What kind of a trick?" Colt asked.

"Not know. Maybe send two riders with two horses each to summer camp to bring more warriors. Maybe split men, let you ride into trap. Cheyenne, tricky."

"Now is where you earn your money, Captain," Colt said. "What are you going to do?"

"Me? I figured you wanted command."

"Hell, no, I'm just an observer. It's your game."

"We ride up and send out some scouts and see what the hell is happening."

They came to the top of the ridge just as the winds blew a bank of clouds away from the rising sun. Binoculars didn't help a lot, but in the edge of the valley a half mile below, both officers saw the Cheyenne. They had herded the 70 or so horses around them, using the animals as a shield.

"That's not going to do much good," Captain Garner said. "How many hostiles in the middle there?"

They could count only about 20 men.

"They could be behind or under horses," Colt said.

"Let's go down to within five hundred yards and see what they do," Captain Garner said.

They spread out in a company front and advanced to 500 yards, then Captain Garner held up his hand and the line stopped.

Below, rifles fired, war whoops stabbed through the air and the army mounts panicked and galloped off in all directions.

Limping Crow laughed. "Aiiiiiiiieeeee. Old

Cheyenne trick. They get close to home summer camp. They give army back horses. We catch horses and Cheyenne get away to save their summer camp."

"Not a chance," Captain Garner said. "Column of Fours!" he bellowed and the troops moved back into fours behind the Captain.

"The Cheyenne will scatter. Limping Crow, pick out one or two and let's follow them. We can get the horses on our way back. I want to pay those bastards back for killing those men back at the fort."

They charged ahead. Now they could see the 20 to 25 Cheyenne scattering as well with the horses. Limping Crow kept moving north, picked out his victims and began tracking them. Soon their prints left those of the army mounts and he pushed ahead faster.

Limping Crow and the two other scouts were 500 yards ahead of the main body when the troopers heard two rifle shots. Captain Garner lifted the troop to a gallop and they surged forward. They came around a small grove of trees and found Limping Crow and one of the other scouts.

Limping Crow lay on the ground beside their horses. "Rear guard," the scout said and passed out. Captain Garner picked out a trooper to stay with the wounded scout and they pressed ahead.

Two hours later the second scout came riding back, a grin on his usually somber face.

"Half hour ahead, Cheyenne camp," he said. "They moving."

"We better hustle up there," Captain Garner said. "We'll gallop a quarter mile and walk a quarter, let's go!"

Well at the back of the ranks the man with the poncho at last took it off and tied it behind his saddle. He still had his hat pulled low and rode a little apart from the others. No one noticed the officer's boots he wore.

First Lieutenant Rodney Strachey gritted his teeth as the word came down that the Cheyenne village was a half hour ahead. He took a firm grip on the reins and kept up with the other troops. He would do what they did, he told himself. He would shoot down the hostiles, he would fight them, he would vindicate himself and prove he was no coward under fire!

CHAPTER ELEVEN

When the A Troop came within a mile of the Cheyenne summer camp, the scouts reported that tipis were coming down and the band was moving.

"Much confusion, women running around, horses running, one hell of a mess," the second lead scout said.

The troops pressed faster.

Captain Garner looked over at Colt as they rode side by side.

"General orders still in force?" he called.

"Damn right!" Colt barked. "Kill the hostile men, capture the women and children, destroy the camp, food supply and horses."

Captain Garner grinned and they charged forward.

There was no time for strategy. The horses topped a small rise and they saw the remains of the Indian camp below them.

"Company front and charge!" Captain Garner bellowed. "Fire at will!"

A Troop swept down on the confused and

harried defenders of Brave Bull's summer camp. Warriors stood and tried to fight. Half of them were mounted and put up a better fight.

Colt saw two troopers go down from gunshot wounds. He knocked a Cheyenne warrior off his horse with a well placed Spencer round, then ducked a lance thrust and pushed the muzzle of the Spencer into the Warrior's chest and pulled the trigger. The Cheyenne's eyes grew wide as his heart stopped beating and he flopped off the side of his war pony never to fight again.

A cavalry attack was always semiconfusion. Once the two forces locked together it became a man-to-man fight. Colt whirled his horse looking behind him just in time to dodge to the side as a Cheyenne arrow whistled past his shoulder. He spurred ahead to a tipi that hadn't been knocked down yet.

Two women ran out, one carrying a child. The older, shorter one held a knife. He looked for other dangers. Most of the fighting had swept halfway through the camp. Colt looked back at the women. One was taller, thinner, her hair chopped off close. Colt looked again. Her hair was blonde.

Captive!

He surged his mount forward, his pistol out now. The Indian woman looked at him, then lifted the knife and drove it forward at the captive female's chest.

Colt fired automatically. The round hit the Cheyenne woman in the chest and drove her back as she dropped the knife. The captive woman's eyes went wide as she looked at him. Her eyes were blue. He rode up, caught her arm, and she vaulted onto the horse behind him. He turned and rode back toward the near side of the camp, saw a trooper nearby and shouted at him.

The private rode over and started to salute.

"This woman was a captive of the Cheyenne. Take her to the rear and see that no harm comes to her. What's your name?"

"Alcott, Sir."

"Your life depends on keeping her safe."

The woman dropped off his horse and vaulted onto the soldier's mount. They rode away from the fighting.

Colt charged into the fray. The riders had worked down the length of the tipi town along the river. Colt rode after them, found a knot of unmounted hostiles behind a bank, and led six cavalrymen to rout them. Three Cheyenne were killed and the other two rushed into the deep woods.

Colt continued downstream and chased the remaining mounted warriors.

There had been no time to detail men to

round up and hold the women and children. Colt saw them vanishing into the trees and heavy brush.

Far behind Colt, Lieutenant Strachey had made it to the very edge of the Indian village. Then something inside him seemed to melt, to cave in, to seep away. He saw a Cheyenne warrior die just in front of him with a bullet through his forehead.

Lieutenant Strachey wanted to vomit. He leaped off his horse as the others charged forward. Death all around him! He hated the dead. He hated death. Why was there so much of it? He saw an Indian woman knocked down by a horse when she darted the wrong way.

She fell, the horse shied to one side and the sharp hoof and shoe came down on the woman's throat, crushing her neck, nearly tearing her head off. Cheyenne blood sprayed on Lieutenant Strachey. He turned, screaming, running, running. He wasn't sure where. He no longer could reason that he was running to or away from anything. He simply ran over bodies, past a horse dying as it pawed the ground, past a burning tipi, near three children who spat and screamed at him.

Then he was by the river. It was soft and gentle and quiet. He sat down and looked at the water. Slowly he crossed his legs and folded his arms and stared at the sacred water, so calm, so controlled. The way he wished he could be.

Lieutenant Strachey at last achieved his Nirvana, his total bliss. The sounds of shooting stopped. There were no wails of the lost, no screams of the wounded or dying.

Peace.

Gentle, soft peace, like a painting of a quiet meadow with a stream wandering through it and a red barn far off at the balance point.

Yes, peace, he said quietly to his inner self.

Then he smiled.

Well down the creek, Colt followed the last of the fighting, and caught up with Captain Garner who had rallied his troops for the move back to the village.

"Knock down the tipis and set them on fire," Garner ordered his troopers. "I want everything here of any value to the Cheyenne burned and utterly destroyed. I don't want to see an unbroken pot or a buffalo robe more than a foot square that isn't burned."

The men rushed around checking tipis, then cutting them down, setting them on fire. They threw the parfleches filled with jerky into the fire and the dried meat burned with a hot flame.

"Casualty report," Colt asked of his Captain.

Ten minutes later the Captain was back where Colt stood beside his mount watching the camp being burned.

"Sir, we have four known dead, possibly two missing, but I'm not sure they ever joined the unit when we left. There are twelve wounded, two seriously, but I think they can ride. We have counted eleven dead Cheyenne, but there may be more in the brush."

"Save four of the long tipi poles and some of the tipi covering. We'll make travois for those two seriously wounded men if they can't ride. Damn lot easier on them that way."

Colt rode around the camp. It was a quarter of a mile long stretched beside the river. He saw a few children searching for the women and the rest of the band. They would find them. It was the warriors of the clan he was angry at. They had attacked a U.S. Fort! It had not happened often in history. No, it was more of a raid, a horse stealing raid. That's how he would report it.

He rode nearly to the close end of the camp when he saw someone by the river. He seemed to be a soldier. Colt rode over and stopped beside the trooper but he didn't move.

Colt stepped down from his mount and squatted in front of the man.

"Good God!"

The soldier was Lieutenant Strachey. He was in another world somewhere. His eyes were glazed and open but in a trance. Colt touched his shoulder, but Strachey didn't notice. Colt shook his head. Strachey had wanted a test, and it looked like he made the test himself — and failed. Damnit!

Colt rode around the burning camp until he found Captain Garner.

"You had one more trooper in your company today you didn't know about — Lieutenant Strachey."

"Not possible, how could he join my troop?" The Captain stopped. "All the damn confusion when we left. Yeah, our men weren't even in squads the way they usually ride. He could have slipped in almost anytime. Is he all right? Did he get wounded?"

"He's as good as he'll ever get. You knew his problem with C Troop?"

"Of course."

"He's sitting over by the river. Go over and see him. I want another officer witness if it comes to that."

It took them another two hours to finish burning the camp. Colt found the trooper he had assigned to guard the woman captive. She sat beside the water, the private nearby. He looked up when Colt rode over.

"She hasn't said a word, sir. She seems to

understand when I talk to her, but she won't speak."

Colt nodded. "Just keep her safe, that's the important thing now. Being a captive of the Cheyenne isn't the easiest experience in the world, especially for a woman."

In the surge to leave the fort, they had provided no rations. Captain Garner saved two parfleches of buffalo jerky and at ten that morning they paused in their duties and ate their fill of jerky and drank pure water from a small spring.

Colt sat beside the rescued woman and gave her a piece of jerky. She ate automatically, but never looked at Colt.

He talked to her gently, softly. "I hope you'll want to tell me your name soon. We'll be here for another hour or so, then move back toward Fort Larson. You're in Wyoming, do you realize that? You're safe now, no one will hurt you. This soldier will defend you. Your ordeal is over now. Just rest and relax. You're going home!"

She showed no reaction. She was blonde, and about five-feet six, tall for a woman. Her hair was ragged as if it had been cut off with a knife. He could see no bruises or wounds on her body that showed around the squaw dress, but he was sure she had been beaten.

All in good time. He remembered Doris

when he first rescued her, but Doris was in much better shape than this woman. Doris had not been a slave. He was sure this woman had been.

The two wounded proved to be unable to ride, and Colt showed them how to make the travois. They used tent ropes to make a loose webbing across the two poles, then covered the rope with buffalo skins and tied them down.

One of the wounded men lay on each travois and one horse pulled the device. The horses objected at first, but with a man in the saddle to guide them, they soon settled into the routine.

Captain Garner decided to move the company back to the site where the Cheyenne had stampeded the army mounts. They would camp there that night and use the rest of the day to round up as many of the horses as they could.

The jerky would sustain the troops for one more day if needed to capture the army mounts. The four dead troopers were tied over horses and put on lead lines. One of the recaptured mounts was saddled and given to the captive woman to ride.

Colt decided to call her Eve, she was like the first woman created.

The roundup was more successful than

Colt had hoped for. They caught and herded together 60 mounts. With the ten they had already caught that meant there were fewer than 20 army mounts still roaming the country. Some of them would come back to the paddock when they realized they weren't getting fed.

Ten more had been seen around town as they came through. The actual loss could wind up being no more than ten.

Colt had made sure that Lieutenant Strachey was cared for. An hour before time to ride out, Strachey came out of his trance, looked around and then shook his head.

"Colonel, looks like I failed my own test. I did it again, didn't I? I retreated inside my own mind and let reality take care of itself."

"I'm afraid you did, Strachey. Now are you ready for that discharge? You'll be able to spend full time on your painting."

"Actually, I'm not that good a painter."

"You can learn, you said you didn't have to sell anything."

"Still, it doesn't seem right. One should be able to produce, to contribute. One should not simply be a sponge living off another's largess."

"Strachey, you'll do fine on the outside. Maybe open an art gallery in Chicago or New York. Sell other people's paintings."

"Yes, yes, I could do that. I think I'd be quite good at that sort of thing."

"Something to think about."

"Yes." Strachey looked away. "Sir, I'd like to get away by myself for a while, think things through."

"Of course."

Colt watched him walk away from their small fire into the night. The man had seemed to accept the reality of his situation. Colt looked at Eve. She had tended their fire, found wood, showed them how to boil the beef jerky to make it more palatable. She had not spoken yet, but seemed pleased that she could be working, doing something with her hands.

Now she had settled down with a buffalo robe she had brought with her. It was old and ragged, but she would not let them take it away from her. Colt also gave her the two blankets off the dead soldiers' saddles.

He had ordered a guard to watch over the woman as she slept.

Later, Colt checked his watch. It was two hours dark by then at just after nine o'clock. Lieutenant Strachey had not come back yet. Colt decided that was understandable. The man had a lot of thinking to do, a lot of new goals to set and new standards. Now he could think of what to do with his life, rather than do what his parents wanted him to.

Colt stretched out on his blankets. It would be a good cool night for sleeping.

Lieutenant Strachey had walked 100 yards up the slight slope from the camp and looked down on 20-odd campfires. It always seemed strange that every two or three men wanted a fire of their own.

He sat on a rock and stared at the blinking lights below.

I'm a goddamned freak of nature, he thought. I'm no good to anyone, least of all myself. I don't want to be an artist. Maybe that's why I'm so bad at it. I really want to be a soldier, to be a General like my father.

Shit! I can't. I won't ever be a General. When we get back to the fort they'll write a report on me, and send me to Omaha where the doctors will ask me questions and say they find nothing wrong. Then the Generals will look at the reports and they will cashier me out of the army. I'll be disgraced. My family will never speak to me again.

Mother will have a spell and take to her bed for a month. I'll not be welcome at the big house in Chicago. My monthly check will stop coming. I'll be begging on the streets.

Strachey took out his revolver and put the barrel in his mouth. It tasted terrible, like metal and bluing and. . . . He pulled it out of his mouth. What else was there? He could go to work in a friend's retail store in Chicago. He could tell his mother he resigned his commission because the army was all politics, not like it used to be. Hard work and loyalty meant nothing these days.

He began to cry. As he did he moved higher on the slope, higher until he could see a small lightning storm 20 miles away across the valley. He found another rock and sat down below it and stared at the dark valley.

The moon was out bright, the storm clouds blown well away. It was a fine night.

Or as the Indians said, "A fine night to die."

He had to make sure. There was no other way. He took out the revolver again and saw that the next chamber had a round in it.

"Goodbye, Mother," he said softly. "Goodbye to all my friends. I won't be seeing you any more. Goodbye, army — my first and only love."

First Lieutenant Rodney S. Strachey put the muzzle of the hand gun in his mouth, pointed it at the top of his head and pulled the trigger.

In the camp below one of the guards looked up. It had almost sounded like a pistol shot, far away. He listened again. There was nothing else. He shrugged. He was still jittery over the action today. It was his first. He had killed his first Indian, and then he threw up. There was more to this Indian fighting than they had told him about.

For a moment he thought he should report the shot. Then he wasn't sure it was a shot. None of the other guards seemed to have heard it. He walked his post and for the rest of his three hours on guard he was especially alert.

CHAPTER TWELVE

Colonel Colt Harding jolted upright on the cool Wyoming valley ground, coming out of a sound sleep to some raucous, ungodly sound. Then he remembered, it was a bugle calling reveille. He hadn't been in the field with a bugle for a long time.

He glanced over at the blankets where Eve had slept and saw that she was up already and had a fire going and had made coffee from the small supply in Colt's saddlebags.

Colt accepted a cup of the hot brew from her. Eve did not look him in the eye, she handed him the cup and scuttled away quickly. He glanced over at where Lieutenant Strachey had spread his blankets. They had not been used. Colt leaped to his feet, slashing sleep from his eyes, pulling on his pistol holster and ramming his campaign hat on his head.

A guard stood 20 feet away. Colt went to him at once. The guard had not seen the Lieutenant.

"Far as I know, no one slept there all night, Colonel," the guard said.

Colt made a fast recon of the small camp. He couldn't find Lieutenant Strachey. Captain Garner swore when Colt told him.

"Goddamn! Where'n hell did he go?"

None of the Sergeants had seen the Lieutenant. Colt set up a search. The men were told to fan out in all directions from the small bivouac, moving on foot, searching every possible spot.

An hour later three pistol shots sounded from almost due east of the camp, up the ridge. Colt and Captain Garner rode up to the spot and dismissed the two enlisted men who had found the officer.

Lieutenant Strachey sat against a rock as if looking out over the valley. The back of his head had been blown away with a round through the mouth. Colt had seen corpses that looked that way before. The service revolver with one round expended had fallen from the dying fingers and lay at his right side.

"Christ, I don't need this," Captain Garner said. He shook his head. "Let's get it official. I invited him to come along as an observer on the raid. After the attack on the village, the Lieutenant was found with a round through his head. Every damn word is true. It will save us all a lot of explaining."

"I'll write the report," Colt said. "No sense in shaming his mother or his family. Every word in the report will be true. Just so some Major doesn't come out from Omaha to investigate further."

An hour later the troop was mounted up and ready to move out. Lieutenant Strachey was tied head down over his horse and added to the other dead on the patrol.

Colt rode next to Eve. She never looked at him, never spoke, did not look at the scenery or the sky. She seemed anxious to stop so she could make a fire or gather wood. She seemed to be ill at ease unless she was doing some kind of work. Colt understood.

Indian women did all the work around the camps. Eve's owner probably beat her if she did not work hard enough or if she stopped. She was showing the effects of many months of conditioning as a slave. She wouldn't lose that ingrained motivation overnight.

Ten troopers drove the herd of horses back south. They kept them closely grouped and had no trouble with strays.

The patrol arrived at the fort after dark that night and were met by half the fort. They stared in sadness at the five men head down over their saddles. None of the men killed had been married.

Colt left the main party and rode with his

hand on Eve's bridle to his quarters. He dismounted quickly and went to help Eve down, but she sprang off the horse before he got there and looked around, but with no obvious curiosity.

Colt reached for her hand, then pulled back. He hadn't touched her. He was afraid she would scream or run if he did. He motioned to her to come with him and she fell into step behind him. At the door to his quarters, she hesitated.

When the door opened Doris stood there all smiles and with a word of greeting that quickly died out. She looked at Eve and knew at once what had happened. She reached out gently and touched Eve's shoulder.

The woman eased back a moment, then looked at Doris's eyes and she must have sensed a friend. She stepped inside and stood there.

Doris spoke with Eve as if nothing was the matter. She talked softly, introduced the children to her when they rushed into the room. They accepted her at once in the wisdom of the young, and hugged their father.

Doris looked at Colt.

"She needs me right now, you'll have to fend for yourself. Eaten supper yet? No, you didn't take any rations. There is fresh baked bread and some ham. I'm going to be busy.

Oh, would you put two buckets of water on to heat for a bath?"

Then Doris vanished into their bedroom with Eve and closed the door. A moment later she came out. "Does she have a name?"

"She hasn't spoken a word since we found her. I've been calling her Eve."

Doris nodded and went back into the bedroom with a stack of clean towels.

Colt ached in every muscle of his body. He hadn't been on a two day trip into the field lately. He put on water to heat first, then played with Sadie and Danny. Sadie said she would get him some dinner. Sandwiches and coffee if he'd fix the coffee. Sadie was going on eight and acting very grown up. At last she frowned at her father.

"That woman, was she with the Indians like I was?"

"Yes, only a different tribe. They were not good to her, treated her like a slave, not a real person. It made her sad and she's not going to be happy for a long time."

Colt stuffed more wood in the fire and sent Danny outside to get another armload. He came back with four small sticks and Colt grinned and helped him with another load.

A few minutes later Doris came out of the bedroom. She blinked and went over to Colt and buried her head in his shoulder. Sobs tore through her and he put his arms around her.

"Oh, God! What did those savages do to that poor woman? She's so frightened, so wary. She's more animal than human. I don't know if she can talk or not, but she hasn't yet. Her hair was chopped off, singed in some places, and her back is a mass of healed scars and welts and bruises. How she ever stayed alive, I'll never know.

"We need something for her to eat. Milk. Is the sutler still open? Could you get another two quarts of milk? He may have some fresh. Milk will be good for her and oatmeal. I doubt if she's had enough to eat for months. She's so thin! She'll need to eat five or six times a day to get her strength back."

Doris dried her eyes, tested the water, then took the round washtub into the bedroom. Colt sat the two buckets of hot water next to the door and knocked.

Colt hurried to the sutler's store at the end of the officers' mess building and bought two quarts of fresh milk and two chocolate bars.

Back in his quarters, he had a sandwich Sadie had fixed for him, then three cups of coffee.

In the bedroom Doris found if she treated Eve like a child it worked better. It took ten minutes to convince Eve that she should take off the squaw dress, and then more time until she would sit in the warm water in the tub. When at last she did, she took the cloth and began to wash herself.

Doris smiled. Some of her old training was remembered. It would come back, she would be well one day. Doris helped her wash her hair. It was still chopped up. Doris was determined to get scissors and a comb and to even it up as soon as she could.

Eve seemed to like the bath. She stayed after she had cleaned herself. At last Doris got the biggest, softest towel she had and held it up. Eve nodded and stepped out of the tub and dried herself.

She looked around, then picked up her old dress. Doris had meant to push it under the bed. Now she shook her head and gave Eve one of her dresses. It had always been a little large for Doris and would fit well.

Doris found some soft cotton underwear and a chemise. Eve put them on slowly, as if trying to remember doing it before. Then she let the dress fall over her head and buttoned up the front of it. Doris put the belt around her and Eve caught it and tightened and fastened it.

Doris sat on the bed and combed Eve's hair. At first she jumped away, but Doris talked softly and at last Eve relaxed and let Doris get the tangles out.

Doris looked at Eve's feet. They were larger

than hers. She had some open sandal-like shoes that might work. She got them from the small closet and tried them on Eve. She frowned and shook her head.

Doris spoke softly and gently tried again. At last Eve stopped objecting and let Doris fit them on her feet. Not the best but they would work until tomorrow. The Sutler had some shoes, she was sure.

Doris put the bath things away and opened the door for Colt to come in and get the bathtub. Eve watched him closely, frowned again, then her face took on the passive expression she usually wore.

"There, now. I think it's time we have something to eat. It's supper time," Doris said.

Doris took her hand and led her out to the kitchen. Eve looked at the small wood cook stove then at the cupboard with utensils and food and her eyes glowed for a moment.

Doris put Eve down at the table and filled a glass with milk and set it before her. At last Eve tasted it, looked at Doris who nodded. She drank half of the glass of milk.

Doris brought out bread and jam and spread a slice. Colt had herded the children into their room as Doris came out with Eve. Now he let them come and watch Eve.

"She's going to be staying with us for a few

months," Colt said. "This nice lady's name is Eve. I want both of you to be especially nice to her."

Colt had brought a folding army cot in from the quartermaster's, and had set it up in the far side of the parlor. He found quilts and spread them on the cot. He put two chairs next to the cot to form a small dresser. It would work for a while. Eventually he thought it would be best to put Eve in the second bedroom with Sadie and Danny on the cot.

For now it would work. He showed Doris the cot and she nodded.

By that time it was nearing ten o'clock. He had put the children down an hour ago. Eve sat at the table watching every move Doris made. When she finished eating she stood and took the dishes to the counter and dipped warm water from the stove into a pan to wash them. "I'll do that," Doris said.

Colt caught Doris's hands. "No, let her," Colt said softly. "She's been working for some Indian warrior fourteen hours a day just to stay alive. She'll want to work, compulsively. She needs to taper off from that gradually."

Doris sat down and stared at the wall. "I remember the work I had to do, and I wasn't even a slave." She shivered. "That poor woman."

"It's going to take a while. We'll just have to be patient. All we can do is hope."

"If it takes a year or two, I'll be here to help her," Doris said. "I have some idea of how she feels."

Colt grabbed his hat. "I've got to check on those wounded men. Be right back."

Outside it was cool and clear. He walked down to the quartermaster building and around to the medical center. Lights blazed from every window.

Dr. Johnson had recruited one of the married enlisted women as a nurse to help him in the medical. The doctor scurried from one small room to another. He paused and looked at the colonel.

"Just told Captain Garner. All the wounded are resting now. One of them I want to send to Omaha where he can get proper treatment. The rest of them will do all right here. Even the Indian is going to make it. Anything else bothering you?"

Colt grinned. "Not much. You heard about Lieutenant Strachey."

"Heard the worst, is it true?"

"Bad as it can get. Going to try to smooth it over a bit."

"Had to put the muzzle in his mouth to do what that bullet did to him."

"That won't be in my report. It will be

151

truthful, but perhaps not all the truth. What I wondered was, could we have saved him?"

"Doubtful. I heard he ran from the fight, blacked out, he called it. Retreated into insanity. When he realized what he had done, he decided he couldn't stand it any more when he was fully conscious. So he ended it."

"At least I know for sure," Colt said. "That puts the final line in my report. Thanks, doc."

"So send me back to Omaha or Chicago and let me work on crazy people. I'd like that. Out here it's blood and guts medicine."

Colt laughed. "Doctor, as I remember you requested a post as far west as you could get."

Doctor Johnson took a turn laughing. "Best way I know to get away from a harpie of a wife. But you don't have that trouble. If some Cheyenne puts a bullet through your noggin one of these days, I've got first rights on Doris."

"I'll tell her that," Colt said. "I'd like you to come over to my quarters sometime tomorrow. I have a friend I want you to see."

"The slave woman? Heard about her. Ideal woman, she doesn't talk. Yes, I'd like to see her. I should check her over medically anyway. Skin and bones, I heard, but that's an easy problem to fix. Not talking . . . well now, that could be something more serious. Then again, she might start chattering away like a parrot any day now."

"Thanks for taking care of these men. You're saving lives out here, doctor."

Dr. Johnson waved, and went back to look at a man who was groaning in the next small room.

When Colt got back to his quarters, Doris handed him a telegram that had just come in. He read it.

CONTINUE TRACK PATROL. MORE INDIAN PROBLEMS ALONG THE RAILROAD. WATCH FOR TRACK AND RAIL DAMAGE. COLONEL HARDING, DON'T WORRY ABOUT THE CIVILIAN TROUBLEMAKER. HE'S HARMLESS. SIGNED GENERAL SHERIDAN.

Colt folded the wire and put it in his pocket. He didn't see Eve. Doris pointed at the cot. She was sleeping.

"She probably has been going to bed when it gets dark and gets up with the sun," Doris said.

"Me too," Colt said. "It's been a long two days."

CHAPTER THIRTEEN

J. Thorndike Dobson showed the telegram to Priscilla. She read it as he paced up and down in front of her in the parlor of her small neat home.

J. T. DOBSON, LARSON CITY, WYOMING TERRITORY. UNDERSTAND YOUR COMPLAINT. IT'S AN ARMY MATTER. MUST GO THROUGH CHANNELS. WILL LET YOU KNOW. SIGNED SENATOR ENGLE BARSTOW. WASHINGTON D.C.

"Isn't that exciting, Thorndike? You received a telegram message from a United States Senator!"

"Priscilla, look what the man says. He says nothing. It's a polite way of telling me to shut up and stop making trouble. He won't even talk to the army about it. He is one of the men who support the army. He won't do a thing."

"Well, I never! He shouldn't say those things in the telegram. I hope you keep it as a souvenir. What are we going to do now, J. Thorndike?"

He paced some more, shook his head. "I certainly am not going to declare war on the army. They have too many guns. I could do what the Indians started two nights ago. I could burn down the whole fort!"

"My, that would be illegal, wouldn't it, J. Thorndike?"

"Yes, Priscilla, it would be. But I'm going to give it a try. Tonight. Do you have any coal oil? A gallon will be enough to start."

"No, J. Thorndike. I won't let you do it. You might get shot and killed. I don't want to lose you. Let's think what else you can do. We can spend the rest of the night trying to figure out what we should do."

She walked toward him unbuttoning her blouse. J. Thorndike watched her. He couldn't move. Another night with Priscilla! That was more exciting than trying to burn out the army. He held out his arms and met her.

It was well past midnight when J. Thorndike lay back on his pillow panting so fast he thought he was going to explode. It just kept going and going.

Priscilla was still panting and glowing. "That was so wonderful, J. Thorndike. You know just what to do, where to touch me!"

155

He heard her, and it pleased him, but he was thinking of something even greater. Yes, tomorrow he would do it and he wouldn't tell anyone, not even Priscilla. She would understand when he came back.

The next day he told his boss at Marshall's Emporium that he needed three days off, some personal business. Mr. Marshall at last said it would be all right.

J. Thorndike fussed around the kitchen putting together some long lasting food in a sack. He took the dozen good six-inch knives and two used revolvers he had bought from the store that morning and put them in another cloth sack. Then he took both sacks with him and went to the livery and rented a horse.

He wasn't the best rider but he could get by. He knew he had to go north, but he wasn't sure just how far.

He rode all day, following the Larson River as it wound up near the Larson Mountains. Then he worked into them, and kept watch. It wasn't until the third day that he saw what he wanted, an Indian campground. He wasn't sure what tribe it was, but it didn't matter.

J. Thorndike lifted a white handkerchief on a long stick he had cut and rode slowly toward the tipis he could see ahead.

He never heard them coming. Suddenly he

was knocked off his horse, his flag, his sack of food and gifts dumped on the ground. He looked up at a steel pointed lance that hovered an inch from his throat.

"Friend!" he shouted. "I'm your friend, I come with gifts for you."

Neither of the Cheyenne understood English, but they did know a murdering White Eye when they saw one. These two warriors were remnants from Brave Bull's band, now staying with White Feather's people 15 miles up the river from their old camp.

One of the warriors jumped off his horse and lifted J. Thorndike to his feet, brushed the dirt off him, then knocked him to the ground with a vicious blow from the side of his lance.

Three times they lifted him up, brushed him off and then knocked him down. At last J. Thorndike pointed to his sacks and made signs he hoped indicated they were gifts.

The warriors dumped out the sacks, found the knives and revolvers and their scowls deepened. They lifted J. Thorndike to his feet and put a rawhide rope around his neck, then rode their war ponies into camp making J. Thorndike either run or be dragged.

Half of the camp turned out to see the parade. Few of them had seen a live White Eye. They stared in surprise and amazement. The warriors brought the White Eye in front of the big tipi of White Feather, the band leader.

White Feather made them wait 15 minutes. J. Thorndike stood in the boiling sun. He had lost his hat. His head was starting to sunburn. He tried to sit down but the tip of the lance dug into his back and he stood again.

When a proper time had elapsed, White Feather came out of his tipi and sat cross-legged in a spot of shade near his shield, lance and bow and arrow. He looked at the two warriors and said a few words.

They chattered back at him. One of the warriors threw his lance, sinking the sharp steel point into the ground three inches from J. Thorndike's foot.

White Feather looked at the guns and knives, then at the White Eye. He asked a question but J. Thorndike had no idea what he said.

"These are for you, gifts to the chief," J. Thorndike said. He made some motions from himself to the chief.

A moment later another warrior stepped into the small circle of men. White Feather said something to him and the warrior turned to J. Thorndike.

"Why you here?" the warrior asked.

"Thank God somebody speaks English!" J. Thorndike said. "I tried to tell them. I'm your friend, I come with gifts, these knives and the two revolvers. Presents to your chief."

One Eared Rabbit turned to White Feather. He had survived the raid on Brave Bull's camp. His wife and a brother died in the fighting. He hated every White Eye he saw.

"This White Eye is here to spy on us for the Pony Soldiers. He says he brings gifts, but I saw him ride with the Pony Soldiers at Brave Bull's camp. He is a spy and will cause the death of many Cheyenne if we listen to his lies."

White Feather looked at J. Thorndike and spat out a few words.

One Eared Rabbit smiled. Two warriors ran up and caught the White Eye.

"What did he say?" J. Thorndike screeched.

"Chief White Feather says you are a White Eye spy, and we will show you what the Cheyenne do with spies for the Pony Soldiers."

The two warriors tore off J. Thorndike's shirt and then his pants. The store clerk screamed at them, tried to fight them off but they knocked him down and held him as they stripped off his short long johns and then his shoes and stockings until he was naked.

Women from the camp began to gather, point at him and laugh. Then the warriors stepped back and the women and young girls ran in and taunted him. They spit on him, scratched him, beat him with sticks. He stumbled backwards, then grabbed at the sticks. But whenever he caught one, a warrior would knock it from his hand with a lance.

An old woman grabbed his penis and pulled it, cackling with laughter. She let go and screamed something that sent the other women into howling laughter.

A young girl ran up to him and flipped up her beaded doeskin skirt, exposing herself to him and laughed. Two girls grabbed his hair and pulled him back and forth. A long stick drew a scratch down his back and blood sprang up.

Now they prodded him forward with the sticks. Sharp points pricked at his skin. One stick whacked his scrotum and he fell down screeching in pain. The women laughed and jabbed at him until he stood. Long red welts and scratches showed down his arms and legs, and across his chest.

A woman ran up to him, bared her breasts and pushed them in his face, then when they touched his face she slapped him six times and backed away braying with delight and derision.

J. Thorndike tried to run between the tipis and get away. A warrior stepped in his path and knocked him flat with the long lance. Before he could get up a dozen small children piled on him, scratching him and hitting him, pulling his hair and pulling at his penis.

He rolled over and sent them flying as he jumped up. The women screeched in delight and moved back to jab at him, make crude sexual suggestions and hump their hips forward in open invitation. He ran at one of the women but she scurried away and the other women grabbed him and spun him around, knocked him down and had him spread eagled on the ground with a woman lying on each of his arms and legs.

One young woman ran up, squatted over him, lifted her skirt and urinated. The yellow fluid hit him on the stomach and sprayed into his face. All around him the entire camp erupted in gales of wild laughter. They pointed at him and bellowed their delight.

The entire camp was enjoying the torture of the White Eye. The sun boiled down. For a moment he felt faint. He knew if he fell down he would die. He had to stay upright. He ran toward a tipi, but a big woman barred the door brandishing a long knife.

He walked back to the beaten grass along the stream, then stepped into the water, but was driven out by two warriors. They herded him into the walkway between the tipis and the women and girls found him again and taunted him, scratched him.

At last he turned and faced them.

"What do you want from me?" he bellowed. "I come as a friend and you torture and torment me. I come in friendship!"

Then the sun was too much, and the emotional strain. He saw the women coming again and he dropped to his knees, then fell on his side, unconscious.

Every voice stilled. The women and girls went back to their duties on skins and food and finding roots.

Two warriors picked up J. Thorndike and carried him into the medicine man's tipi. They splashed cold water on him to awaken him, then stood him up and painted him with seven different colors.

"Water," he said. Then made a drinking motion. One warrior brought him a bowl of water and he drank as much as he could hold not knowing when he might get any more.

When he was painted the seven colors of the seven spirits, he was led to the center of the camp and tied to a tree that had been peeled of its bark. His hands were fastened so high over his head that he could stand, but do little else. He was still naked.

Now the women did not touch him or strike him with sticks. They could only spit on him. A few small girls tormented him, but soon they went off to play in the stream.

A dozen eight- to ten-year-old boys whooped around with small bows and arrows, and played a game seeing who could shoot his arrow closest to the White Eye without hitting him. No one stopped them.

The tree was in the middle of the camp and the sun hit it fully. It was called the truth tree by the Cheyenne.

The warrior came by who spoke English. He stopped and stared at J. Thorndike.

"You were stupid to come here with such a story. I knew you were a spy for the Pony Soldiers."

"No, no!" J. Thorndike screeched. "I hate the soldiers. I come as a friend. I brought knives and guns to you. Would a spy do that? I come as a friend."

"Then you are too stupid to live. You do not matter. Not even the White Eyes will worry about a man so stupid as you. After twenty-four hours on the tree of truth, we will know for sure why you were sent here. No longer will your tongue be able to lie as it does now."

The warrior stared at him a few moments more, then he moved on.

J. Thorndike could not believe it. The women were savages! They could have killed him if they had wanted to. He had never been so violated, so tortured in his life. These people had no concept of friendship. How could he be a spy?

A small boy's arrow sailed toward him and hit his chest. It had no point and no power and fell to the ground. The boy who hit him with the arrow lost the game and had to pick a new one. The boys ran to the stream and began throwing water at the girls playing there.

J. Thorndike felt the sun beating down. He tried to move to a comfortable position but there was none. He felt a wave of lightheadedness sweep over him. It passed. Then it came again and he felt it deepen and his vision clouded and then everything merged into a blackness as he passed out.

J. Thorndike sagged against the tree, only his hands holding him up.

One Eared Rabbit watched from in front of his tipi. He drank deeply from a water jug as he watched the White Eye spy faint. By this time tomorrow his tongue would be thick and he would not be able to lie. Then they would discover why the spy had been sent from the Pony Soldiers.

CHAPTER FOURTEEN

In just two days at the fort, Colt could see the difference in Eve. She still didn't talk, but her eyes were starting to lose the haunted, hunted look. She darted around the quarters less, and now and then she would sit in a chair and look out the window.

But mostly she worked. Twice on the second day she was there she scrubbed the kitchen floor. She washed out the two dresses she had worn and hung them to dry in the doorway. She made the fires, did any cooking she could.

Eve watched Doris, learned what she did quickly and repeated it almost exactly. Eve didn't have to be shown how to do something more than once. Every morning she braided Sadie's long blonde hair.

It seemed she enjoyed this activity the most. Sadie liked it too, and talked a purple streak whenever Eve braided or brushed her hair.

Once Doris saw Eve look at herself in the

mirror in the bedroom. She touched her face, then her hair, and quickly looked away and began to sweep the bedroom floor.

Twice a day, Doris sat down with Eve and read to her. She held one of Eve's hands so she would stay in the chair. At first Eve paid no attention, then gradually she began to listen and for a while Doris thought she was interested in the story of the novel Doris read.

More than once Doris had blinked back tears. She remembered the Indian camps, she had seen one slave woman. She had been so thin and sickly that she simply died one day. Her body had been carried into the brush far enough from the camp so she wouldn't be smelled and dumped there like a dead dog.

She had been a Mexican woman who spoke only Spanish. Doris had asked White Eagle about her, but the band's leader had simply shrugged. She was no concern of his, she was a slave and whatever her owner did with her was his right.

Daily Doris was amazed that Eve had kept herself alive. She had no way of knowing how long Eve had been a slave of the Cheyenne. A year, two years, three years?

The routine at the fort continued about the same. The daily patrols went out and checked the tracks. There had been no activity found along the 20 miles each way from Fort

Larson. Another north patrol had not found any Indians deeper into the valley.

Colt had not heard anything on his requested promotion of Sergeant Troob to Second Lieutenant. He wondered what Department Headquarters was doing with the paperwork. Any day he expected the papers to come back marked unapproved and with a letter of chastisement.

He had written a letter to the next of kin, Lieutenant Strachey's mother. He had been brief, told her part of the truth so it jibed exactly with the official report of his death. The officer had been buried quietly in the small cemetery at the edge of the fort.

Just after noon, the Larson County Sheriff came to see Colt. He was a large man with a heavy moustache, high cheekbones and deep set eyes that seemed to watch everything at once.

"Colonel Harding, don't think we've met," the man said holding out his hand. It was rope scarred and rough. An ex-working man's hand.

"Name's Oxe, Rufus Oxe. I got elected sheriff when nobody else in the county wanted to run. Now I see why."

"Sheriff, good to meet you."

"Wondered if your men had stumbled on a body or any sign of a missing man I have reported. His name's J.T. Dobson. Hear he was harassing the troops the other day."

"Dobson, yes, I've met him. A rather intense young man. Thinks all Indians are saints and we're the bad guys."

"Dobson is an asshole, but usually he don't get in no trouble. His boss said he asked for three days off to take care of some personal business. Then I find out he rented a horse the same day and said he'd be gone for three or four days. Time's up and he ain't back."

"Sorry, Sheriff Oxe, no reports of a wandering horse or dead body. But we'll keep a watch. Any idea which way he went?"

"He said something to the hostler about a long ride. No idea which direction. Could have gone to Denver, for all I know."

"We'll keep a look out."

"Colonel, folks have a way of taking things for granted. I'm just damn glad that you and your men are here. Protecting the tracks and all that, but you keep the Cheyenne pushed back a good ways from the town, too. Was a time that we had some hostiles coming damn near into town. Now things is mostly quiet."

He shook Colt's hand and wandered outside.

Major Longley came in with the letter Colt had asked him to write. It was an official request for four more officers to bring them up to full strength.

"Won't get them, but time to try again," Longley said. Colt signed the letter and looked at his organization chart. They needed the four men for the field companies and troops.

Then he was thinking about Dobson. He didn't know why. Where would the man go? Relatives, business, Cheyenne maybe? He shrugged it off. That was one problem he didn't have to worry about. Eve was worry enough. He hoped that after two or three more days she would open up and start talking.

This noon she had watched him warily. Colt was careful not to make any sudden moves around her. Now she trusted Doris and the kids, but she was still not sure about Colt. He was a man. Men had hurt her. It made sense.

A rider came in from one of the patrols. The south and east unit had run into a band of about 20 Arapahos. They had been digging on the tracks and the patrol flushed them away and gave chase. One Indian was listed as dead and one trooper wounded.

The cavalryman fell from his horse when it went down with a rifle round in its head. The trooper suffered a broken leg.

There was no real damage to the roadbed, but the station master at Larson City depot had been notified.

The next day the patrol moving north reported that someone had felled trees into the Larson River and dug a ditch out of the bank and diverted about half of the water against the right of way and had washed out a 20-foot-long section of tracks.

The westbound train had to be held up at the Larson City station for six hours until the tracks could be repaired and the fill dirt brought in to reestablish the tracks and the grade.

Far to the north of Fort Larson, J. Thorndike Dobson sat in the medicine man's tipi. His hands and feet were both tied with rawhide. He was still naked. He had seen his clothes burned in a fire. The colors he had been painted with he realized were some kind of stain.

Only the stain had saved him from blistering in the sun while against the truth tree. J. Thorndike wondered why he was still alive. The 24 hours standing and hanging by his hands were the worst he had ever experienced. His wrists and arms ached. He could not lift his right arm above his waist.

His tongue had become so swollen that he

couldn't talk. After they cut him down from the tree they had rolled him in the river for an hour to help him recover. He drank too much water and had cramps and threw up. But he wouldn't admit that he was a spy.

"I come in peace and friendship, I come with gifts for the great chief."

But each time he tried to tell White Feather these things, the interpreter, One Eared Rabbit, turned around what he said and made the White Eye sound more and more like a spy.

"Why are you keeping me alive?" J. Thorndike asked the medicine man. He was a small person who could only use one arm and had long ago been damned to be "with the spirits" because now and then he would fall to the ground, his body would writhe and chatter and he would foam at the mouth and swallow his tongue. When he had these visitations of the spirits the whole camp stopped all activity and they watched and waited for him to recover from the wrestle with the spirits and tell them what he had learned.

Every time he had a new insight. Each time he had some good news for the camp. Twice he almost died during the fights with the spirits.

The medicine man's name was Shaking Bear. He had taken the name after his first wrestle with the spirits. He also had learned some English when he was at one of the forts with a peace commission from Washington.

Now Shaking Bear watched J. Thorndike. "You not spy. Much dumb." He shrugged. "But White Feather want spy, Brave Bull wants spy. You spy."

"Why are you letting me live?"

"Test of three spirits," the medicine man said. But he would say no more about it.

All afternoon J. Thorndike sat there pondering it. When One Eared Rabbit came with food for him that evening, he asked the warrior about it.

One Eared Rabbit grinned at the question.

"Yes, three tests to see if you truthful. White Feather wants be sure you are spy."

"What are the tests?"

"First, wailing rock. You tied on big rock at dusk. Great spirit must protect you from Brother Bear, from coyote, from vulture and hawks, from snakes and all night creatures that love to eat Indian and White Eye flesh."

"Silly superstitions. What's the next test?"

"Wait until you pass first test, then I'll tell you. It will happen tonight. You will be smeared with buffalo fat and honey to attract the animals. Perhaps a hill of fire ants will find you."

"Not unless you put them there."

"Most pass first test of spirits. Not many pass second."

"Most animals are afraid of man, they won't attack man unless they are starving. What's the second test?"

"Better don't know."

"I come as a friend, can't you believe that? Why do you hate all white men so much?"

"Your Pony Soldiers attacked Brave Bull's camp few days ago. My wife, my brother, both killed by Pony Soldiers. That why I hate Pony Soldiers. You help them!"

"No. I hate what the soldiers are doing to the Indians. For the past year I have been trying to help you. I've written letters to Washington, to the President, to Senators. I'm pleading with them to stop killing Indians. Last week I marched in front of the fort to keep the soldiers from riding out. They stripped off my clothes the way your people did."

"White Eye lie! White Eye no damn good!" One Eared Rabbit stood and hurried out of the tent as if he could not stand to hear that any white man had tried to help the Indians.

J. Thorndike watched Shaking Bear who had not said a word while the warrior was in the tipi.

"You're going to kill me, aren't you?" the prisoner said. "You love to torture people, so

173

you stretch it out as long as possible. I'll pass the first test, maybe the second, but on the third one I'll die. I know that now. I've learned a lot about the Cheyenne these past few days. Damn, was I wrong about the noble American Indian. I was dead wrong.

J. Thorndike almost laughed at that bad pun. But if he started to laugh he was sure he would never stop — not until one of the warriors came in and killed him. No, he couldn't laugh. Not yet. Not yet.

He smiled at the medicine man. "You are extremely kind to permit me to live so long, Shaking Bear. I appreciate your generosity and your thoughtfulness."

Shaking Bear frowned at the White Eye. Confuse him, J. Thorndike thought. Confuse him and smother him with kindness. It just might throw him into another of his fits. Then there might be a chance for him to get to a knife and escape. Maybe.

CHAPTER FIFTEEN

At breakfast, Eve was up before the rest of them as usual, had the fire going and coffee made. She was drinking coffee now as well and seemed to enjoy it. She hadn't spoken yet.

She brought Colt his breakfast, two eggs fried sunnyside up over a plateful of potatoes that had been sliced from last night's boiled potatoes and fried with three strips of bacon. She had washed the top of the stove in back and brought a pair of slices of toast turned to a golden brown.

A moment later she brought Doris a bowl of oatmeal with milk and brown sugar. Then when she was sure both were pleased with their food, she sat down with a small bowl of oatmeal and a piece of toast with only butter on it.

"I swear, Eve, I don't know what we did around here before you came," Colt said softly. "You do things here in the house so fast and so well, that sometimes I wish I had you running my office. We'd be a lot more efficient, I'm sure."

Eve looked up at Colt and the edges of a smile showed around her face. She looked over at Doris who was smiling broadly. Then Eve looked down.

"First time," Colt said softly to Doris. They smiled their secret. Yes, there was still hope.

It was nearly ten that morning when Sergeant McIntyre knocked on the Colonel's door and pushed it open.

"Sir, a man is here to see you. Said it was important. He's just arrived from up in Cheyenne country."

Colt sat up straighter and grinned when the man came in the door. He wore buckskins with uneven fringes that Colt bet the man had tanned and worked out himself. A little squaw probably did the stitching and sewing. He wore winter moccasins, leggings and a fur cap even though it was the middle of summer. The Spencer repeating long rifle seemed glued to his right hand as he came in.

"Sir, this is Lefty Ashwood and he says he never lets that rifle out of his sight."

"It's all right, Sergeant," Colt said, standing. He held out his hand. "Mr. Ashwood, looks as though you know what a mountain and an open campfire is all about."

"Yep, Colonel, suh, I been known to light a

fire or two. Like the pup said there, I do some work with the Cheyenne. Feisty lot, but they do need a trader and that's me, usual. Sometimes they just as soon shoot at me as trade, but we usual work things out. Got me a Cheyenne woman way up there, so they look on me more like kin."

"Coffee?" Colt offered.

"Middle of the morning you folks drink coffee?" Lefty asked. "Saw it happen once in Omaha."

Sergeant Mcintyre brought in two cups of coffee and the mountain man sipped it, then grinned.

"Wouldn't know how to like coffee if it wasn't burned a little. Good." Lefty wiped his nose with his thumb and finger and cleaned the residue off on his pants leg.

"Dang near forgot a minute. Came in to tell you some news. You got a white man missing hereabouts?"

"Fact is, we do. A towner."

"Figures. Just come from up on the Larson, way up. Gent named White Feather. He's got a bulging summer camp. Seems like some cavalry bunch jumped on Brave Bull's camp and wiped it out. So them still alive went up to White Feather's place.

"Ain't the story I was tellin'. They got this White Eye, poor sombitch called Dobson.

From what I hear he comes a'riding right up to the camp just proud as you please with some knives and a couple of old pistols as a peace offering.

"Mood ain't too good for peace up in there nowadays, not after Brave Bull getting his hind-side whacked and eighteen showing up dead. They stripped this little sombitch and gonna be putting him through the tests from what I hear."

"When was that? How long ago did you see Dobson alive?"

Lefty scratched his arm, then his crotch as he stared at the ceiling. "Two days ago. Yep, I moved right along considering there might be a reward for this dumb-assed white fart."

"No reward. Sheriff didn't mention any. What's the talk up there? Why are they keeping Dobson alive?"

"Unusual. They say he's a spy for you Pony Soldiers. That's why I come here. He working for you?"

"No. He's a pacifist. Wants to shake hands and dance with the Cheyenne."

"He's been dancing a damn strange tune so far. They stripped him naked and painted him seven colors for the seven spirits."

Colt paced his office. "Are they waiting to see if we follow him and attack them?"

"Bout the size of it." Lefty held up his cup.

"That pup got any more of this boiler juice?"

When the mountain man's cup was filled, Colt stopped in front of him.

"Plain that the army can't go in there with a fighting force or Dobson would be killed first shot."

"He ain't one of yourn, why you worrying about him? Dumb-assed fool to ride into a Cheyenne camp alone."

"Lots of them kind of fools around here, Lefty. How long do you think Dobson can last up there, before they get tired of playing torture games with him and toast him over a fire?"

"Four or five more days from when I left. He'd already been there three days way I could figure."

Colt stepped back and tamped his pipe full and fired it. When it was burning good enough to last, he looked back at the trader.

"You came down to get some specific item to trade with, I'd guess. What are you looking for?"

"Axes and saws. Damn Cheyenne suddenly figured out that it's less work to saw down a tree with a White Eye bucksaw or crosscut than it is to chip away at it with a stone axe."

"Getting too smart for their own good. How many axes you need?"

"Ten would do me proud, and two bucksaws, all broken down, course."

"You're talking seven dollars worth of goods at the town emporium. Would you lead me back up to that camp as a paid army scout at a dollar a day for seven days work?"

"Hell, yes. Them Cheyenne ain't gonna lift my hair. Yours looks right smart the way it is. Why you aiming to get it cut off?"

"Not planning. I've been in and out of an Indian village or two before. Walked in alone to Chief Red Cloud's camp one day and he almost dropped his breechclout."

Lefty shook his head. "Ain't accusing you of lying, Colonel. But what you just said is one hell of a lot easier to talk than to do."

Colt unbuttoned his shirt and stripped it off and turned his back to the trader.

"Holy shit! Is that what it looks like it is?"

"It is. Never thought I'd live through it. You have the same scars?"

"Not a chance. *Okepa*, Christ! That's nothing I want anything to do with. They hung you by two pegs skewered through the skin on your back, right? Then to make it hurt more they hung buffalo skulls on your ankles. How long did they hang on, twenty minutes, half an hour? You pass out? The four I saw do the ritual passed out in twenty minutes." He looked up at Colt. "Let's see your left hand."

"They didn't chop off a finger on me," Colt said. "Special favor to me from Red Cloud. If

I get caught, those scars make me blood brothers with half the tribes on the plains."

"Damn well better. You died once. Never met a white man before who went through *Okepa*. Hell, I'll guide you any damn place you want to go."

"I want to go in and bring out Dobson."

"How many troopers going with us, a battalion?"

"Just you and me, Lefty. Can you be ready to leave in two hours?"

"Peers as how. Just us two, huh. Hell, why not? You have the axes and saws?"

Colt called in Major Longley and explained the situation.

"I need seven dollars cash for the scout. Don't tell anybody where I'm going, especially not Doris."

Lefty grabbed the money and headed for the door. "Can I trade in my horse? He's sturdy, just worn out from a fast trip."

"Yes," Colt said.

Two hours later Colt went for a ride out the paddock side of the fort and met Lefty in town. Colt wore a pair of well worn buckskin pants, a fringed shirt and a civilian wide brimmed hat. He had his Spencer and a pair of ivory handled Colt revolvers.

Lefty looked at him a minute then nodded.

"Damn right. Figured I should have heard

about that *Okepa* story before. I have. They used to call you Captain Two-Guns. Peers as how you got promoted."

"Happens," Colt said. "Two days to get up there? We have to make it in a day and a half or better yet, before it gets light tomorrow morning. You've got a good horse, and we're going to push both of them to the limit. I figure a horse isn't as important as a man, any man, even Dobson."

Colt held the horses to a six miles per hour gait as they sped up the river. Lefty knew where to take short cuts and they moved gradually to the right closer to the mountains where the Larson River would come back into them. After four hours they gave the horses a rest and washed off in the river.

"Whatever happened to them Lightning Troops you used to train?" Lefty asked.

"Still around. Didn't feel we needed one here. I was probably wrong."

"At least two tribes I worked with were scared as hell of the Lightning bunch. One old chief said the Lightning troops were as good at being Indians as the Indians."

"We worked hard at it," Colt said. "I'd reckon you are about two thirds Cheyenne yourself for sneaking up on a passel of the red men."

Lefty chuckled.

They rode again. It was dark before they had to shift into the trees to escape detection. They passed near where the fight had been with Brave Bull's band.

"About fifteen, eighteen more miles," Lefty said.

They had to slow in the dark, and it was almost 11 o'clock that night when they came to a point that Lefty said was less than a mile from White Feather's main camp. They found a spot of heavy brush and worked their way into it and made a quick camp. Colt fried up steaks he had brought with him packed in ice from the Larson City ice house.

They slept.

Colt was up with the sun. They had worked it out on the ride. Colt would shadow Lefty on the last mile to the camp. He would leave the horses well back and scout out the situation.

Colt said he understood that Lefty could not be in on the rescue. "I don't want you jeopardizing your standing with the tribe, that's vital to you. But, if you could stage some kind of a contest or a game —"

"How about an axe throwing contest down at the far end of the camp away from the medicine man's tipi. That's where Dobson is. They'll keep him there until the final test. Course it might have started by now."

"What's the third test?"

Lefty shifted on his saddle. "Ain't pretty. Could be any of three or four, every one of them is guaranteed to wind up the man dead and past time for burying. Just ain't pretty at all."

Colt took the horse from Lefty and gave him a 20 dollar gold piece. It had been agreed. Colt needed another horse to get Dobson out on. Lefty could spin a yarn about how his horse broke a leg and he had to shoot it a day's walk back.

Colt now followed through the heavy trees above Lefty as he strode through the small valley near the Larson. It was larger here, with two or three tributaries emptying into it before it added its water to the North Platte. The bundle of axes and saws was over his shoulder and a small bag of "possibles" tied around his waist. Lefty carried his trusty Spencer rifle in his right hand.

A half mile from the main camp a lookout challenged Lefty.

Lefty yelled at him in Cheyenne dialect and the young Indian man laughed and passed him along.

Colt found a spot for the horses a half mile out and caught up with Lefty. He kept to the heavily timbered slopes of the ridges, but so he could spot Lefty moving along.

Then Lefty entered the camp shouting to people he knew. Colt began to work his way down toward the camp. If they had scouts out along the river, they could have one on each side. It depended on how frightened of the army they were.

He moved slowly, listened and watched, but he could find no scouts on this side of the river. Foot by foot, Colt worked down toward the camp. He had left his Spencer on his horse. If he got into enough trouble to need it, he was dead anyway. This had to be a quiet, quick snatch and be away.

After two hours he was within 300 yards of the nearest tipis. He had angled toward the far end where the bigger tipi than most had a painting of a bear's head on one side. That would be home for their medicine man, Shaking Bear.

Colt lay still in the mulch of the woods and watched the tipi. After two hours he saw a small man whose left arm hung uselessly at his side walk out of the tipi. Behind him came two warriors with Dobson between them. He was still naked, and the paint still looked colorful over his body.

The warriors led Dobson toward a cleared place 30 feet from the tipi under large trees. It had two nooses hanging down from overhead branches. Colt watched the warriors. They were taking Dobson to the start of a test. Colt just hoped that he wasn't half a day too late!

CHAPTER SIXTEEN

Colt Harding lay there in the brush less than 50 yards from the Cheyenne camp watching helplessly as the two warriors lifted Dobson and snared his ankles in the noose and left him hanging upside down, his head a foot from the ground. His arms were tied securely to his body. Another man was brought out. He was hung in the same manner six feet away at the next noose, his head three feet off the ground where a small fire had been laid. His arms also were tied tightly to his body with wet rawhide.

Colt sucked in his breath. Brain Boil! He had heard of it but not seen it more than once. It wasn't pretty as Lefty had said. The braided rawhide ropes around the men's ankles were played over a limb and tied to the tree trunk. Each rope could be used to raise or lower the head above the fire.

Now Dobson was hoisted up four feet off the ground and two women came in and laid a fire directly below his head but did not light it.

The medicine man marched out in a special robe of pure white fur that Colt couldn't identify. He carried a burning stick and with many incantations and formal rituals walked around the circle that surrounded the hanging bodies. He went up to each man's fire and pretended to light it, then darted back. At last with a mighty scream he lit the fire of the second man.

The fire flared up brightly for a moment, then burned down and as it did Colt could tell the man was another Indian, probably a captive from another tribe who would not work as a slave. He would be sacrificed to the spirits to bring the band good fortune.

As the fire burned brightly, the naked Indian's long hair smoked and then caught fire. The man screamed as his hair quickly burned off his head. Colt had to look away. Black wisps of smoke curled from the man's blackened skull. As the fire reached its peak the Indian fainted.

A woman stepped up and threw a gourd full of water into the Indian's face. He came conscious with a long, low wailing scream of absolute terror and realization.

Without warning the rope pulled the man well above the fire. The heat hardly touched him now. Small bits of wood were added to the fire constantly to keep it at the same heat level.

The Indian man twisted and turned to try to see the white-robed medicine man.

Colt watched Dobson. He was shaken, it was plain to see. Tears streamed down his forehead from his eyes. His hair hung straight down toward the unlit stack of firewood below him. Colt could almost feel his panic. When would they light his fire? When would he start to heat up and when would his hair burn off?

Without warning the rope lowered the Indian over the fire again, this time a foot below the previous level. Colt couldn't stand to watch the Indian's eyes. They were alert, frantic as he looked around. Then in a matter of seconds, it seemed that his eyes went glassy, that he stopped twisting and swinging.

The fire below burned as hot as ever, searing the skin on his scalp. Soon the skin began to char. The Indian gave a scream, then the sound cut off and there was no movement whatsoever from the victim.

J. Thorndike Dobson watched, the horror growing in his mind. What could he do to stop this? How could he get out of it? When would they light his fire? He twisted and saw One Eared Rabbit and called to him, but the interpreter did not hear, or pretended not to hear.

Dobson decided that he would confess that

he was a spy. He knew where the Pony Soldiers were and he could lead the Cheyenne in a surprise raid and trap them in a small canyon where they hid. But he had to get someone's attention.

"I am a spy!" he bellowed at last. "I am a Pony Soldier spy and can lead you to their hidden camp."

One Eared Rabbit heard and came toward him, careful to stay out of the circle the medicine man had drawn.

"Too late, White Eye spy. You are going to boil your brains out like this Arapaho spy we caught. Your hair singes off, then your scalp burns and at last your brains boil and your skull explodes like a ripe melon!" One Eared Rabbit glared at Dobson, then turned and walked away.

Dobson now looked and saw hundreds of Indians standing around the circle watching the execution. Everyone in camp must be there.

He heard a strange noise and looked at the Arapaho beside him. He could almost feel the heat of the other fire. The noise came again, then blood seeped out of the Indian's ears.

Dobson turned his face away, then closed his eyes. But he had to look back. Blood ran out of the Indian's nose, then his mouth. His eyes bulged, then blood came out his ears in a stream.

For a moment Dobson thought he would vomit. There was nothing in his stomach to come up. He watched, in deadly fascination now, unable to tear his glance from the body not six feet away.

The sound came again. Dobson knew what it was. The Indian's brains and blood in his skull were boiling! How long could that go on? He had to be dead, dead some time ago.

It sounded like a pistol shot. The Indian's skull exploded. A weak portion over the left ear blasted outward toward Dobson. Hot blood, brains, bits of skull and tissue splattered over Dobson. He retched, his body heaving but nothing came up.

Dobson thought he would die right there. He looked at the Cheyenne and saw the intense concentration on the people's faces. Warriors, old women, men, young boys, girls carrying babies, all watched, fascinated as they crowded around closer and closer to the circle.

When the Arapaho's skull exploded there was a long let out gasp. The Indians watched the corpse for a moment, then began to fade away.

Someone shouted at the far end of the camp. Dobson couldn't tell what was going on. Soon the only other person at the ceremonial circle was Shaking Bear.

There were more shouts from far down at the other end of the quarter mile of tipis. He heard challenges, and shouts of victory.

Curiously something moved in front of him out in the brush beyond the camp. He blinked blood off his eyes and stared harder. A figure moved in short bursts from tree to tree until he was near the edge of the ceremonial circle but still concealed in the brush.

A white man! Dobson didn't believe it.

The figure in the white fur robes stood, lit a stick from the fire under the dead Arapaho and moved slowly toward Dobson's ready made bonfire.

The man at the edge of the circle leaped forward, raced a half dozen yards, a knife flashed across the medicine man's throat and the old man fell. Blood gushed into the dirt of the ceremonial circle.

The white man lunged forward, leaped and sliced at the rawhide rope that held Dobson up. He slashed it again, cut through it and caught Dobson before he fell. He turned Dobson right side up.

The man dressed in buckskins cut loose the noose from Dobson's feet and at once started him running for the woods. Dobson tried to move, but his feet and legs were paralyzed from lack of blood. The big man picked up Dobson, lay him over his shoulder and ran into the dense brush. He kept running for a quarter of a mile, then dropped to the ground and untied Dobson's arms.

"Glad you were second on the exploding skull program today, Dobson," Colt said.

Dobson got a good look at the man. He didn't believe it.

"Colonel? Colonel Harding from Fort Larson?"

"So far that's my post. Could be hell if we don't get out of here. In a few minutes we're going to have about eighty-five furious Cheyenne warriors on our trail. The horses are another quarter of a mile. Can you walk?"

He tried. He could. Then he ran. They made it to the horses before they heard the screams of protest far behind them.

Colt boosted Dobson onto the mount, then they rode south. Colt worked them along the ridge angling away from the river and the easy route.

On the way up, Lefty had told Colt about a cave approximately three hours from the village. It would serve them well if they could find it. With every Cheyenne in the area looking for them, they would have little chance of outrunning the searchers.

The Cheyenne would use their two horse

system, riding one horse until it nearly dropped while leading another mount. Then they would trade to ride the fresh horse trailing the used one until it regained its wind. They could travel remarkably fast that way and outrun any single mounted man.

Colt found the first landmark and turned up a small feeder stream. The second point to look for was less than half a mile away.

Colt could hear Cheyenne calling to each other as they fanned out in their search. They must be tracking them as well. He came to the shallow creek and both rode up it for another half mile, then angled around a lightning scarred tree.

"Wait!" Colt barked. They both held still. Far down the small valley they saw three horsemen coming toward them. The riders flared one to each side of the valley, the third man right straight up the center.

"What now?" Dobson asked. He was still naked, still stained seven colors and splattered with a dead man's brains and blood.

"The last one who can see us will enter that brushy spot, then we go across the creek. I see what I've been missing. That brush near the face of the little cliff. We ride right through it. Now!"

They rode across the creek at a walk, over some sheet rock to the brush. Colt nudged into it and it parted, he rode forward. It was a screen of brush in front of a cave. A moment later they were inside. Colt saw that the cave was maybe 20 feet deep with a cleft somewhere to the front that let in light.

"Take the horses to the back of the cave and tie their muzzles shut with the reins. I'm going to wipe out some foot prints."

He edged out of the cave into the brush, broke off a piece on the inside and looked out downstream. For a moment he saw no horsemen. He darted out beyond the flat rocks and brushed out the hoof prints of the two horses, then brushed out his own as he backed into the sheet rock and hurried inside.

Far below he heard an Indian cry, and then another. He squeezed through the brush leaving it as natural looking as possible.

Both men sat there and watched as a dozen Cheyenne soon came splashing up the creek. A cry brought the Indians to a halt as they found some fresh hoof prints. Two warriors jumped down and began to track the horses, but ten feet from the water they lost the track. It was where Colt had rubbed out the prints with the piece of brush.

Colt held his breath as one of the Indians looked directly at the brush that concealed them. He started toward it, but a voice from the other side of the stream called, and he turned away.

Soon the trackers were pounding downstream, hoping to find a place where the two White Eyes had left the water and moved away through the hills where they could be tracked.

Colt took a deep breath as the last of the Cheyenne rode away. He went back in the cave and dug a pair of army pants and a shirt out of his saddlebags. On the other horse was a pair of boots. He handed them to Dobson who had started to shiver.

"Colonel, I don't see how I could have been so wrong about the Indians."

Colt held up his hand and motioned for the man to get dressed. "Right now we have to get away from those former friends of yours. We'll stay right here until it gets dark, then we'll ride due west and see if we can put some distance between ourselves and those hostiles. I don't think that you want me to take them on single handedly, and you don't have any weapons."

Dobson sat down on the ground. He shivered, then he gasped a dozen times and shook his head.

"You had anything to eat lately?" Colt asked.

Dobson shook his head.

From his saddlebag, Colt took a chocolate bar and gave it to Dobson.

"Don't look like much, but it's pure energy. And soon as it gets dark we're going to need all we have. I figure there must be two or three ridges between us and the big valley. Then we'll swing wide around to the far side of the valley and ride south until it gets near daylight. We'll hide out until night again. That second night we should be able to get back to the fort."

"If the Cheyenne don't find us first."

"Right now that's a damned big 'if.' Why don't you lay down on the blankets off the saddles and try to get some sleep. We'll be riding as soon as it gets dark. From what my timepiece says, that should be about seven tonight. It's not quite noon now. Try to sleep."

Colt took one of the blankets and settled down near the opening of the cave. He could at least hear if any Cheyenne came their way. They might and they might not. That one warrior could decide to check out his hunch. He had looked like he wanted to investigate the brush closer.

Dobson went to sleep almost at once.

Colt drowsed, slept by fits and starts.

Suddenly he was wide awake. A horse nickered outside. Colt came up with his knife in his right hand and a pistol in his left. He crouched next to the opening, out of sight. If the warrior found the cave he would have to come through the brush and be out of sight of any other Cheyenne with him.

Colt listened. He sensed more than saw someone nearby. Outside the brush rattled, then crackled again as someone parted it. Colt could see the light come through, then a shadow. The figure moved forward and Colt knew that his eyes had not adjusted yet to the dim light.

Colt's advantage. He saw the warrior clearly now, a rifle in his hands. Colt drove forward with the knife in his outstretched stiff right arm like a spear. The blade drove deep into the warrior's chest. Colt sliced it outward and heard a death rattle as the Cheyenne fell at his feet.

Colt cleaned the blade on the dead Indian's shoulder, then stepped to the brush screen and parted it just enough to see through. A lone war pony stood outside. There was no chance that he could catch the war pony. It would run from a stranger. Yet it would stay there waiting for its master.

Colt moved to the other side where the brush was thicker and worked his way out so he could see downstream. Nothing. There were no more Cheyenne that he could see for half a mile.

He checked his watch. It was a little after five in the afternoon. How soon would the dead warrior be missed? How and who would search for him?

Cheyenne warriors were supposed to take care of themselves. There would be no search for him until well into the morning, or maybe a day later. They should be safe in the cave for another two hours. Colt hoped the Cheyenne had not told anyone where he was going. If he had kept his own little secret, it might be just the break they needed to get away clean.

Two hours later no other Cheyenne came. It was almost dark outside when Colt roused Dobson. At first he thought he was still a captive, then he cried for a minute, regained his composure and led his horse toward the entrance.

He saw the Cheyenne's body and stopped.

"Oh, God, you killed him."

"True. I figured that was better than letting him kill both of us. Let me go outside and see if we have any more visitors."

Colt stepped through the brush and scanned the little valley in the quickly approaching dusk. He saw only trees and grass and a gently flowing stream.

A moment later he and Dobson were riding up the side of the ridge, moving due west.

Colt had studied the stars for a moment, found the north star from the big dipper pointers, and picked his line of march.

Now all they had to do was avoid half the Cheyenne nation and then maybe, just maybe, they would see Fort Larson again.

Maybe.

CHAPTER SEVENTEEN

Twice early that evening they heard calls that Colt figured were Cheyenne shouting from one ridgeline to another. They were still looking. They knew if they didn't find their quarry during the night it would be too late.

For three hours Colt pushed the horses due west, over three ridges, then at last down into the gentle valley. He wasn't sure if they were in the top of the Larson River plain, or the adjoining one formed by the Medicine Bow River.

Either one was fine with Colt. They rode an hour into the summer grass and then turned south. The moon was out nearly full and there were no clouds. Colt picked up the pace from the walk they had been on and made better time.

Not once had Dobson complained or asked to stop. Colt knew he was hurting, but he kept it inside. The man had learned a lot in the last few days. He would never forget hanging upside down next to that Indian when the man's skull exploded.

Colt did not recognize any of the country they rode through. By midnight they were well away from the mountains on the broad valley. They kept riding.

Twice they stopped to rest the horses. Colt found himself dozing in the saddle and saw that Dobson was doing the same. He found a small stream with plenty of brush around it, and just before daylight, they stopped for a rest. They tied the horses and Colt waited until full light and looked around.

Dobson had rolled out his blanket and slept at once.

Colt studied the land in every direction. There were no settlers in this area yet, only the unbroken virgin land extending as far as he could see. A paradise, but with a deadly stinger in its tail called the Cheyenne.

He figured they better sleep here a while. At the pace they were traveling, even without Cheyenne around they could fall asleep on their horses, fall off and break their necks.

He settled down, spotted a rabbit eating a morning meal, and dropped off to sleep.

Colt awoke four hours later, rested, ready to ride. He looked out from the brush and trees at the flat valley. He could see five miles behind them, six or seven across the gently sloping valley to the ridge lines.

If a band of Cheyenne did spot them, they could outrun the hostiles with a five mile start. He decided to risk it and ride south; Dobson was up a moment later and they each ate a chocolate bar from Colt's saddlebags and drank all the water they could hold, then rode south.

There were no more surprises and they came into Larson City just before dark. At the back door to the Emporium they stopped and Colt held out his hand.

"Dobson, I'm glad I got you out. There was nothing else I could do. Lefty saw you, without him we couldn't have done it."

Dobson shook the strong hand gladly. "I . . . I don't know what I can say. I was a fool. I won't give you any more trouble, you can bet on that. Thank you, Colonel Harding, for saving my life. Now I'll have to see that I do something to justify my own existence."

Colt rode back to the fort, trailing the second horse. He turned them in at the paddock and walked wearily to his quarters.

Doris had heard he was back and stood outside the door as he walked up. She put her arms around him and hugged him, then kissed him.

"You never did tell me where you were going."

"Didn't want you to worry. Tell you about it tomorrow. I need some food and a soft bed." He grinned. "I'll get to you tomorrow night."

She held him a moment. "We've got a new member of our family. I got him mostly for Eve and she's taken to him like a mother hen. Come look."

Inside the quarters Danny and Sadie rushed to him. He carried them into the living room where he saw Eve sitting in a chair watching a summer fire in the fireplace. On her lap was a small bundle of fur. She looked up, smiled and stroked the brown haired puppy.

"Captain Barnholdt's dog had pups and they were big enough to be weaned. Emily was giving them away and I figured that Eve . . . well, I was right. She loves that puppy."

Colt explained quickly where he had been.

"You went alone again? You could have been killed up there, you know that? You've got to stop playing the hero." She sighed. "I know, a white man was a captive and you knew what the Cheyenne would do to him and you had to get him out. I surrender."

After a big supper, Colt had a bath and went right to bed. He slept until ten o'clock the next morning.

Back at his desk, Colt caught up on the

fort's business. Still no word from Omaha on his field commission for Troob.

"What are they doing, actually considering it?" Colt wondered out loud. Major Longley laughed.

"Good to have you back. There's a dispatch there you're not going to like. I've seen this guy operate before."

Colt read the dispatch. A Major Parsons was coming out to do a final investigation of Lieutenant Strachey's death.

"This means the man really did have connections. Damn unusual for somebody to come from division to check into a battle death."

"Strachey was a damn unusual man. Not much else going on. Regular patrols routed another batch of Arapaho getting ready to mess up the tracks. Generally it's to the east side."

"We'll manage. The alert is still on, then."

Major Longley sat down in the chair beside Colt's desk. "About time you told me about your one man army trip into the Cheyenne camp."

Colt told him. "So we made it back, and didn't compromise Lefty. Damn, I don't ever want to see a skull explode that way again. I can't describe the sound."

"I guess Dobson won't give us any more trouble."

"He's going to forget the word Indian completely. He's cured for life."

Major Parsons arrived on the morning train. He was a small man with a trimmed moustache, almost bald and carried a swagger stick like a weapon.

He introduced himself and took a sheaf of papers from a small leather folder he carried. They sat in Colt's office and Major Longley was with them.

"This report on Strachey seems complete enough. There is no real problem. Frankly, we got pressure to come out and do a more complete investigation. Turns out that Strachey has an uncle who is a U.S. Senator with strong ties to the army. He's yelling at us to dig deeper."

Colt shifted in his chair and looked at his adjutant. Major Parsons caught the exchange. "Gentlemen, this report can be interpreted several ways. It says the officer was killed by a round to the head while on a patrol chasing a Cheyenne band who had attacked the fort. It doesn't say that the Cheyenne fired the fatal shot."

Colt stood and leaned on his chair. "Major, have you ever been in an attack on an Indian village?"

"No, sir, Colonel, I haven't. But I did put in four years of fighting in the Civil War."

"Good. Then you know the absolute confusion of battle. There is no way to say what bullet killed who when the graves registration people move in to take care of the dead and wounded. Don't you agree?"

"Yes. I support you one hundred percent. But in many cases there is evidence of how a man was killed. I have a vague feeling here that you gentlemen know more than went in the report."

Colt sighed and sat down. He called Sergeant McIntyre to bring in coffee and the special cinnamon rolls that Eve had made early that morning.

"You're right, Major. There is more to the story, but we felt that it was better to word the report this way. Lieutenant Strachey had twice before frozen up or run away from fighting with Cheyenne. He said he blacked out and had no memory of doing anything wrong. But he could not remember the fighting in either case.

"I had relieved him of command and asked him to resign. When the Cheyenne raided the fort, he joined the patrol going out. It was put together quickly and there was a lot of confusion. We didn't know he was along. When the fighting started he rode away, sat down beside a stream and turned within himself. He simply ran away from reality because it was too hard for him to face.

"When I found him I told him what had happened. He seemed to accept it. Said he would resign and become an artist. He admitted his father had been a General during the war, but was dead now and his mother was all army.

"That night at our camp he said he needed to be alone a while. He went off and I wasn't worried about him. We found him the next morning with a round through his mouth that blew off the back of his head."

Major Parsons rubbed his face and groaned. "Goddamn. So everyone in the fort knows what happened."

"Impossible to keep something like that from the men."

"I'll try to cap it right here. I'll write another report that comes directly from the field and the officers. involved. That should keep the Senator off our backs. The only way he'll ever find out differently is if he comes here and talks to the men himself. He's too busy to do that."

"Major, I hope so. The report we sent is factual and accurate as far as it goes. We saw no need to destroy an older woman by finding out her son was a coward."

"We could write him up for a medal," Major Parsons said. "That would help settle it.

How about a medal of honor?"

"Absolutely not," Colt said. "That would cheapen it too much."

"The Certificate of Merit Medal, then. It's been around a while and carries some honor. Would you accept that?"

Colt sighed. "Yes, if you think that will settle the matter once and for all."

"I do. I'll talk to the Senator in person and put it all to rest." The Major sipped at his coffee, then smiled. "Oh, one more item. I'd like for you to bring a Sergeant Troob here so I can talk to him."

"Troob?" Major Longley asked.

"Yes, I believe he's a First Sergeant."

The adjutant went into the other room and had Sergeant McIntyre send for the man.

Back in the office, the officers talked about the weather, the state of the Indian wars, and what General Sheridan had been planning next for the campaign against the hostiles.

Then the door opened and Sergeant Troob walked in. He snapped to attention and saluted.

"Sergeant Troob reporting to the Commanding Officer as ordered, sir."

"Good morning, Ted," Major Parsons said. "Been a damn long time since I've seen you."

Troob looked then at the Major and his

208

face broke into a smile. "Charlie . . . Major Parsons!" He took the offered hand and shook it.

"Ted, I didn't even know you were back in the army. Last I knew. . . ."

"Yes, but I'm back. I really didn't like it on the outside. So here I am."

"Ted, I brought you something. Not much, but it's a start, and knowing you, I'm sure you won't have these for long."

He took out a pair of Russian pattern shoulder knots with First Lieutenant's gold bars on them.

"First Lieutenant Troob, you are hereby re-commissioned a First Lieutenant in the United States Army, which is a permanent rank. Congratulations, Lieutenant Troob."

Troob brushed wetness from his eyes, then shook hands with the Major.

"Sorry about this little surprise, Colonel. But I served as a Second Lieutenant under Colonel Troob during the big war. Finest damn officer I've ever met. Just glad I could be the one to bring his shoulder boards and his Russian knots."

Both Colt and Major Longley congratulated Troob.

"I've also brought orders for the Lieutenant to be transferred to Division Command in Chicago until we find exactly the right spot for him. You'll be leaving with me on the evening train, Lieutenant Troob."

"Yes sir," Troob said. He smiled. "Damn! I never thought it would happen. Phil Sheridan must have pulled some strings."

Major Parsons laughed. "Wouldn't hurt to set him up to a drink or two when we get to Chicago."

Troob came to attention. "Gentlemen, I have some items to take care of, some packing and some goodbyes."

"We'll have an official presentation ceremony at three this afternoon," Colt said. "Longley, will you pass the word? All troops will fall out for a promotion ceremony."

"Yes, sir."

Colt grinned. "This has turned out to be just one hell of a good day after all. Major Parsons, you're welcome to use my desk to write up your second report on the Strachey affair. I have an appointment."

Colt walked out of his headquarters grinning. He saluted two surprised privates as he made his way to his quarters. The first person he wanted to tell was Doris.

When he opened the door to his quarters, Doris ran into his arms. She was crying.

CHAPTER EIGHTEEN

"Doris, what's the matter?" Colt asked softly. His wife leaned back and he could see a smile coming through her tears. She slipped away from him and motioned for him to follow her.

They went to the living room door and looked outside. Eve was sitting beside Sadie combing her hair.

"Some day I'm going to have a little girl just like you, Sadie," Eve said. "She might not be as pretty as you are, but she'll be almost as nice. We haven't figured out what to call our puppy yet, have we?"

Colt pulled Doris back to the kitchen.

"She took a nap this morning just after we had a snack. We've been eating five or six times a day. She got up after her nap and came out and asked me where I had put Sadie's comb. She wanted to know if she could use it.

"I started to cry and she looked at me and asked me what was the matter. It was as if she had been talking all her life."

"Then we shouldn't tell her she didn't talk for a while. We should be careful about that. Have you asked her name yet?"

"No, I called her Eve and she looked up, but she didn't correct me. Let's see how she reacts to you."

They walked up into the living room. Sadie left Eve and ran to her father who picked her up and gave her a big hug and a kiss.

Colt turned to Doris. "Oh, my big news. Sergeant Troob is now First Lieutenant Troob. A major came from Division today and brought his re-commission and his new orders."

"That's great!" Doris said. "You knew he was wasted as a Sergeant."

Colt looked at Eve. "And where is that puppy today? Not chewing up my slippers, I hope."

The young woman grinned. "I hope not, too. Oh, you've been calling me Eve. That's close but my real name is Elmira. Elmira Rowland."

"Well, Elmira, that's good to know. Now are you two going to get me some dinner here or not?"

Elmira grinned and hurried toward the kitchen and Doris went with her. Colt felt a strong sense of satisfaction. She was talking!

Now they could find out where she came from, and see if she had any kin around. Likely the county sheriff in her original place could help them. No, she could tell them herself now!

After the dinner, Colt held the puppy. "Elmira, we're not sure where your people are. Do you have any relatives?"

"Yes, of course. I live, no, I lived, on a farm in western Nebraska. I have a sister in Omaha on Belmont Street, but I'm not sure of the number. Yes, three-fifteen! That's it. I can write her a letter."

Colt wrote down the address and slipped it in his pocket. He would send a telegram as soon as he got back to the office.

"What's your sister's name, Elmira?"

"Susan. Susan Fuiten. She's married to an undertaker of all things. I haven't seen her in over a year. She'll be surprised to find me here in Wyoming Territory."

Colt sent the wire as soon as he got back to the office. He expected a reply back quickly, maybe even that same afternoon, depending on when the message was delivered in Omaha.

"If a wire comes in from this Mrs. Fuiten, I want you to bring the message to me, no matter what time it is," Colt told the key operator.

The promotion ceremony went exceptionally well. Lieutenant Troob's troop clustered around him after it was over. They congratulated him but were sorry to see him leave.

"No wonder I never really liked you," one private said. "You was a damn officer all the time just pretending to be a Sergeant." Everyone laughed.

That night around the fire, Colt decided he had to bring up Elmira's captivity.

"Where did you live in Nebraska?" he asked.

"Out near Scottsbluff. We had a farm. I'd only been married about two months. Then they swept down on us." Elmira stopped and wiped her eyes.

Doris nodded. "I can still remember the terror of those first few minutes when they attacked our place."

"They burned down the barn and the house," Elmira went on. "I guess they must have . . . have killed Ben somewhere. I never saw him. They took our three horses and killed our cow and then they tied me on a horse and we rode away."

Doris touched her hand. "It's good to talk it out. Talk it out and deal with it. You know that of the five of us in this room, Colt is the only one who has never been a real captive of the Indians."

"Actually, I was a prisoner for a while with

Red Cloud. I couldn't leave until I proved my bravery. I finally got free."

Elmira looked around and smiled and wiped away the tears. "I . . . I think I'll be all right now. It's been so long since I've felt safe, since I've known for sure that I would live to see another day."

A knock came on the door. Colt went to it and came back. He had an envelope. It was addressed to Elmira Rowland. He carried it in and held it a moment.

"Elmira, this noon I sent a wire to your sister. She must have received it in Omaha. This looks like an answer to it. It's addressed to you."

Elmira took the envelope and stared at it. She put it down on her lap and glanced away, then looked back.

"What if she says she doesn't know me and never wants to see me again? I've heard stories about rescued women who had been captives of the Indians. How the other women snub them and treat them so bad."

"Those are just stories," Doris said quickly. "Look at me, I'm the Colonel's lady. If anyone treats you bad, tell me and I'll pull her hair out!"

That brought a smile to Elmira. Slowly she tore open the envelope and unfolded the piece of paper that was printed in pencil as the

215

letters came in over the wire.

She read it, then bent low and began to cry. Doris put her arm around Elmira.

"Nobody is going to hurt you, Elmira. We're here. We're your friends."

She looked up and shook her head. She couldn't speak. She gave the wire to Doris who read it out loud.

"TO ELMIRA ROWLAND, FORT LARSON, WYOMING. ELMIRA. GLORIOUS NEWS. WE WERE AFRAID FOR YOU. WONDERFUL TO HAVE YOU ALIVE AND WELL. I AM COMING TO LARSON CITY ON THE MORNING TRAIN. ARRIVES THERE NEXT DAY. CAN'T WAIT TO SEE YOU. WE ALL LOVE YOU. SIGNED SUSAN FUITEN.

Colt brushed some wetness from his eyes and went to the kitchen. He would write a follow up report on Elmira for Division tomorrow. Times like this made all of the work and sweat and danger out on the frontier worth while.

Colt went back into the living room. He caught up the children and took them into the bedroom and read them a story.

When he went out the two women were busy in the kitchen. Work was what had brought Elmira back from the edge of insan-

216

ity. Work would sustain her.

Colt sat down and filled his pipe. He had his work as well. The Cheyenne and the Arapahoes would keep him busy for some time. But he would stay at the fort as long as the army wanted him to. He liked the garrison life for a change. There would be Indian trouble for years.

Maybe sometime in the future General Sheridan would have another special assignment for him. He would accept it. Until then he was going to relax, do his job here at Fort Larson, and enjoy his family — while he could.

We hope you have enjoyed this Large Print book. Other Thorndike Press or Chivers Press Large Print books are available at your library or directly from the publishers.

For more information about current and upcoming titles, please call or write, without obligation, to:

Thorndike Press
295 Kennedy Memorial Drive
Waterville, ME 04901
Tel. (800) 223-1244
Tel. (800) 223-6121

OR

Chivers Press Limited
Windsor Bridge Road
Bath BA2 3AX
England
Tel. (0225) 335336

All our Large Print titles are designed for easy reading, and all our books are made to last.